Jack stood up, and suddenly all she was breathlessly aware of was those sexy blue eyes watching her.

He was so close now she could hardly breathe, and he gave her that smile that always made her insides tumble.

He put a hand under her chin and lifted her face to his. 'I'll cook dinner and you can wear the dress. You don't need a babysitter.'

Her heart was thumping in her chest and her whole body throbbed with a sexual awareness that was totally unfamiliar. 'You hate this dress.'

'I never said I hated the dress.'

Their eyes locked and suddenly all she could think about was that kiss. The way it had felt when his mouth had claimed hers.

She wanted him to kiss her again.

LAKESIDE MOUNTAIN RESCUE—

romance and drama that will keep you on the edge!

*Siblings Bryony, Tom and Oliver Hunter are
members of the Lakeside Mountain Rescue Team—
they're willing to risk all, ready to save lives!*

*And as winter approaches and
the weather worsens their skills, and their emotions,
are about to be tested to the limit...*

*Don't miss these three exciting novels
from Medical Romance™ starting with:*

THE DOCTOR'S CHRISTMAS BRIDE...**In
November 2004**: Bryony Hunter has been in love with
A&E consultant Jack Rothwell for most of her life, but
to him she is his best friend. So she decides that the
time has come to date other men. And suddenly Jack
starts to see her in a different light.

In December 2004 meet GP Oliver Hunter. He is
waiting for Miss Right, but when he finally meets her
she's seriously on the rebound after a disastrous break-
up. How is he going to prove to her that she can love
again so soon?

In January 2005 it's Tom's story. Tom Hunter broke
up with Sally Jenner seven years ago, to concentrate on
his career, and now she's back in his life. Despite the
uncontrollable passion between them, she makes it
clear that she isn't going to trust him with her heart
again. But Tom has other ideas...

THE DOCTOR'S
CHRISTMAS BRIDE

BY
SARAH MORGAN

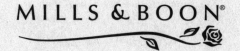

All the characters in this book have no existence outside the imagination of the author, and have no relation whatsoever to anyone bearing the same name or names. They are not even distantly inspired by any individual known or unknown to the author, and all the incidents are pure invention.

First published in Great Britain 2004
Harlequin Mills & Boon Limited,
Eton House, 18-24 Paradise Road, Richmond, Surrey TW9 1SR

© Sarah Morgan 2004

ISBN 0 263 83932 X

Set in Times Roman 10½ on 12¼ pt.
03-1104-45262

Printed and bound in Spain
by Litografia Rosés, S.A., Barcelona

PROLOGUE

'MUMMY, I've written my letter to Santa.'

Bryony tucked the duvet round her daughter and clicked on the pink bedside light. A warm glow spread across the room, illuminating a small mountain of soft toys and dressing-up clothes. 'Sweetheart, it's only just November. Don't you think it's a little early to be writing to Santa?'

'All the decorations are in the shops. I saw them with Grandma.'

Bryony picked up a fairy outfit that had been abandoned in a heap on the floor. 'Shops are different, Lizzie.' She slipped the dress onto a hanger and put it safely in the wardrobe. 'They always start selling things early. It's still ages until Christmas.'

'But I know what I want, so I thought I might as well write to him now.' Lizzie reached for the stuffed mermaid that she always slept with. 'And anyway, this present is special so he might need some time to find exactly the right one.'

'Special?' Bryony gave a groan and picked up the book they'd been reading all week. 'Go on.' Her tone was indulgent. 'Hit me with it, Lizzie. What is it this time—a horse?' She toed off her shoes and curled up on the end of her daughter's bed with a smile. This was the best time of the day. Just the two of them, and Lizzie all warm and cuddly in her pink pyjamas. She smelt of shampoo and innocence, and when she was tucked up in bed she seemed younger somehow, less like a seven-year-old who was growing up too fast.

'Not a horse.' Lizzie snuggled down, her blonde curls framing her pretty face. 'Bigger.'

'Bigger than a *horse*?' Bryony's eyes twinkled. 'You're scaring me, Lizzie. What if Santa can't find this special present?'

'He will.' Lizzie spoke with the conviction of youth. 'You said that Santa always gives you what you ask for if you're good.'

'Ah—did I say that?' Bryony took a deep breath and made a mental note to concentrate more when she answered her daughter's questions in future. 'Well, it does depend on what you ask for,' she hedged, and Lizzie's face fell.

'You said he *always* gives you what you ask for if you're good.'

'Well, he certainly does his best,' Bryony said finally, compromising slightly and hoping that the request wasn't going to be too outlandish. Her doctor's salary was generous, but she was a single mother and she had to watch her expenditures. 'Do you want to show me this letter?'

'I've sent it already.'

'You've sent it?' Bryony looked at her daughter in surprise. 'Where did you post it?'

'I went into the post office with Grandma and they said that if I posted it there it would go all the way to Santa in Lapland.'

'Oh.' Bryony smiled weakly, her heart sinking. 'So it's gone, then.'

Which meant that there would be no chance to talk

Lizzie out of whatever it was that she'd chosen that was obviously going to cost a fortune and be impossible to find in the wilds of the Lake District.

Bryony sensed a trip to London coming on. Unless the internet could oblige.

'Uh-huh.' Lizzie nodded. 'And he's got until Christmas to sort it out.'

'Right. Are you going to give me a clue?'

'You'll like it, I know you will.'

'Is it something messy?'

'Nope.'

'Something pink?' Everything in her daughter's life was pink so it was a fairly safe bet that whatever was top of her Christmas list would be pink.

Lizzie shook her head and her eyes shone. 'Not pink.'

Not pink?

Feeling distinctly uneasy, Bryony hoped that her mother had managed to sneak a look at the letter before it was 'posted' otherwise none of them were going to have the first clue what Lizzie wanted for Christmas.

'I'd really like to know, sweetheart,' she said casually, flipping through the pages of the book until she found where they'd left off the night before. She wondered whether the post office had binned the letter. At this rate she was going to have to go and ask for it back.

'OK. I'll tell you, because it's sort of for you, too.'

Bryony held her breath, hoping desperately that it wasn't a pet. Her life was so frantic she absolutely didn't have time to care for an animal on top of everything else. A full-time job and single parenthood was the most she could manage and sometimes she struggled with that.

A pet would be the final straw.

But then she looked at Lizzie's sweet face and felt totally overwhelmed by love. More than anything she wanted her daughter to be happy and if that meant cleaning out a rabbit…

'Whatever it is you want,' Bryony said softly, reaching out and stroking her daughter's silken curls with a gentle hand, 'I'm sure Santa will get it for you. You're such a good girl and I love you.'

'I love you, too, Mummy.' Lizzie reached up and hugged her and Bryony felt a lump building in her throat.

'OK.' She extracted herself and gave her daughter a bright smile. 'So, what is it you want for Christmas?'

Lizzie lay back on the pillow, a contented smile spreading across her face. 'A daddy,' she breathed happily. 'For Christmas this year, I really, *really* want a daddy. And I *know* that Santa is going to bring me one.'

CHAPTER ONE

'Six-month-old baby coming in with breathing diffi-culties.' Bryony replaced the phone that connected the accident and emergency department direct to Ambulance Control and turned to the A and E sister. 'That's the third one today, Nicky.'

'Welcome to A and E in November.' The other woman pulled a face and slipped her pen back in her pocket. 'One respiratory virus after another. Wait un-til the weather gets really cold. Then everyone falls over on the ice. Last year we had forty-two wrist frac-tures in one day.'

Bryony laughed. 'Truly?'

'Truly. And you wouldn't laugh if you'd been working here then,' Nicky said dryly as they walked towards the ambulance bay together. 'It was unbe-lievable. I wanted to go out with a loudhailer and tell everyone to stay at home.'

As she finished speaking they heard the shriek of an ambulance siren, and seconds later the doors to the department crashed open and the paramedics hurried in with the baby.

'Take her straight into Resus,' Bryony ordered, tak-ing one look at the baby and deciding that she was going to need help on this one. 'What's the story?'

'She's had a cold and a runny nose for a couple of days,' the paramedic told her. 'Temperature going up and down, and then all of a sudden she stopped taking any fluids and tonight the mother said she stopped breathing. Mother came with us in the ambulance—she's giving the baby's details to Reception.'

'Did she call the GP?'

'Yes, but he advised her to call 999.'

'Right.' Bryony glanced at Nicky. 'Let's get her undressed so that I can examine her properly. I want her on a cardiac monitor and a pulse oximeter—I need to check her oxygen saturation.'

'She's breathing very fast,' Nicky murmured as she undid the poppers on the baby's sleepsuit. 'Poor little mite, she's really struggling. I suppose we ought to call Jack—even though calling him will massage his ego.'

Bryony looked at the baby, saw the bluish tinge around her lips and heard the faint grunting sound as she breathed.

'Call him,' she said firmly. 'This baby is sick.'

Very sick.

She didn't care if they massaged Jack's ego. She trusted his opinion more than anyone else's and not just because he was the consultant and she was a casualty officer with only four months' A and E experience behind her. Jack Rothwell was an incredibly talented doctor.

Nicky finished undressing the baby and then picked up the phone on the wall and dialled, leaving Bryony to carry out her examination. She watched the baby breathing for a moment and then placed her stethoscope in her ears, strands of blonde hair falling forward as she bent and listened to the child's chest.

When she finally unhooked the stethoscope from her ears, Jack was standing opposite, looking at her with that lazy, half-bored expression in his blue eyes that always drove women crazy.

And she was no exception.

She'd known him for twenty-two years and still her knees went weak when he walked into a room. She'd often tried to work out why. Was it the sexy smile? The wicked blue eyes that crinkled at the corners when he smiled? The glossy dark hair? The broad shoulders? Or was it his sense of humour, which had her smiling almost all the time? Eventually she'd come to the conclusion that it was everything. The whole drop-dead-gorgeous, confident masculine package that was Jack Rothwell.

When she'd started working in A and E in the summer, she'd been worried about how it would feel to work with a man she'd known all her life. She was worried that finally working together would feel odd. But it didn't.

She'd fast discovered that Jack at work was the same as Jack not at work. Clever, confident and wickedly sexy.

'So, Blondie,' his deep masculine tones were loaded with humour. 'You need some help?'

Blondie…

Bryony grinned. He'd called her 'Blondie' when she'd been five years old, and now she was twenty-seven he was still calling her 'Blondie'. She'd even had a brush with being brunette at one point in her teens but it had made no difference. He'd still called her 'Blondie'. It was one of the things she loved about their friendship. The way he teased her. It made her feel special. And, anyway, it meant that she could tease him back.

'This baby's sick.'

'Which is presumably why she's in hospital,' Jack drawled, leaning across and reaching for her stethoscope, the fabric of his shirt moulding lovingly to the hard muscle of his shoulders. Despite his teasing words his eyes were on the baby, looking, assessing, mentally cataloguing his findings.

Bryony watched him with admiration and more than a touch of envy. His instincts were so good. If anyone she loved ever ended up in A and E, the doctor she'd want them to see would be Jack. He had a brilliant brain and an amazing ability to identify medical problems based on seemingly scanty information. And she'd learned more from him in her four months in A and E than she had from any other doctor in her career so far.

'So what did you notice, Blondie? Apart from the fact that there's a little patient on the trolley?'

He stood back while Nicky attached leads to the baby's chest and connected them to the monitor.

'She's cyanosed, has intercostal recession and she's grunting,' Bryony said immediately, her eyes on the baby. 'Her resps are 60 per minute and she's becoming exhausted.'

Jack nodded, his eyes flickering to the monitor, which was now operational and giving them further clues to the baby's condition.

'She has acute bronchiolitis. We need to get a line in this baby fast,' he ordered softly, holding out a hand to Nicky who immediately proffered the necessary equipment. He handed it to Bryony. 'Go on. Impress me.'

'You want me to do it?' Bryony looked at those

tiny arms and legs and shook her head. 'I'd rather you did it.'

She could see how ill the baby was and she didn't have the confidence that she'd get the line in first time. She knew Jack could. And with the baby that sick, his skill was more important than her need to practise.

His eyes narrowed and his gaze was suddenly serious. 'Don't doubt yourself,' he said softly, his blue eyes searching as he read her mind. 'Do it.'

He was still holding out the equipment and Bryony sucked in a breath. 'Jack, I—'

'Can do it,' he said calmly, those wicked blue eyes locking on hers. 'In three months' time you're going to be working on the paediatric ward and you're going to be taking blood all the time. You need the practise. Go for it.'

Bryony hesitated and Jack lifted an eyebrow, his blue eyes mocking.

'You want me to hold your hand?' His voice was a lazy drawl and Bryony blushed. How could he be so relaxed? But she knew the answer to that, of course. During her time in the A and E department she'd learned that panic did nothing to improve a tense situation and she'd also learned that Jack's totally laid-back attitude to everything rubbed off on the rest of the staff. As a result, they operated as a smooth, efficient team.

Looking at the baby, Bryony bit her lip and lifted the child's tiny wrist.

'Relax. Take your time.' Jack closed long, strong fingers around the baby's wrist and squeezed. 'OK.

Here's one for you. What do you call a blonde with half a brain?'

Bryony was concentrating on the baby's wrist. She found a tiny, thready vein and wondered how she was ever going to hit such a tiny target. It seemed almost impossible.

'Gifted,' Jack said cheerfully, squinting down at the baby's hand. 'You'll be fine. She's got good veins. Stop dithering and just do it.'

So she did and the needle slid smoothly into the tiny vein on her first attempt.

Relief and delight flooded through her.

'I did it.' She looked up, unable to hide her pride, and Jack smiled, his eyes creasing at the corners.

'As I said. Gifted. Now you just need the confidence to go with it. You're a good doctor. Believe in yourself.' His eyes held hers for a moment and then he looked at Nicky. 'OK, we need a full blood count, U and Es, BMG, blood culture and viral titres. And Nicky, let's give the child some humidified oxygen.'

Believe in yourself.

Well, she did believe in herself. Sort of. It was just that she was afraid of making a mistake and Jack Rothwell never seemed to be afraid of anything. He just did it. And it turned out right every time.

Bryony busied herself taking the necessary samples. 'Should I do arterial blood gases?'

'They can do them on the ward,' Jack said immediately. 'Nicky, can you call Paeds and get them up here? This little one is going to need admitting. She's a poorly baby.'

Bryony looked at him. 'You think it's bronchiolitis?'

'Without a doubt.' He smothered a yawn and looked at her apologetically. 'Sorry. I was up half the night.'

It was Bryony's turn to look mocking. 'Was she nice?'

'She was gorgeous.' He grinned, that wonderful slightly lopsided grin that affected her knees so acutely. 'She was also eighty-four and had a fractured hip.'

'You love older women.'

'True.' He checked the monitor again. 'But generally I like them mobile. OK, Blondie. What's the likely causative organism here? Exercise your brain cell and impress me twice in one evening.'

'RSV,' Bryony said immediately. 'Respiratory syncytial virus causes 75 per cent of cases of bronchiolitis.'

He inclined his head, his expression mocking. 'All right, you've impressed me. And you've obviously been studying your textbook again. Now we'll do some maths. What's two plus two?' His eyes were dancing. 'No need to answer immediately and you can use your fingers if you need to. Take your time— I know it's tricky.'

'No idea,' Bryony returned blithely, batting her eyelashes in a parody of a dumb blonde and handing the bottles to Nicky for labelling. 'Jack, should we pass a nasogastric tube?'

'No. Not yet.' He shook his head, his gaze flickering over the baby. 'When you've finished taking the samples we'll set up an IV and get her to the ward. I've got a bad feeling about this little one. She's going to end up being ventilated.'

'I hope not,' Bryony murmured, but she knew that Jack was always right in his predictions. If he thought the baby was going to need ventilating, then it was almost certain that she would.

He looked at her quizzically. 'Is the mother around?'

As he asked the question the doors to Resus opened and the paramedics came back in, escorting a tall woman wrapped in a wool coat. Her face was pale and her hair was uncombed.

'Ella?' She hurried over to the trolley, her face lined with anxiety, and then she looked at Jack.

Bryony didn't mind that. She was used to it. Women always looked at Jack.

Even before they knew he was the consultant, they looked at him.

And it wasn't just because he was staggeringly, movie-star handsome. It was because he was charming and had an air of casual self-assurance that attracted women like magnets. You just knew that Jack would know what to do in any situation.

'I'm Dr Rothwell.' He extended a hand and gave her that reassuring smile that always seemed to calm the most frantic relative. 'I've been caring for Ella, along with Dr Hunter here.'

The woman didn't even glance at Bryony. Her gaze stayed firmly fixed on Jack. 'She's been ill for days but I thought it was just a cold and then suddenly today she seemed to go downhill.' She lifted a shaking hand to her throat. 'She wouldn't take her bottle and she was *so* hot and then tonight she stopped breathing properly and I was *terrified*.'

Jack nodded, his blue eyes warm and understanding. 'It's always frightening when a baby of this size is ill because their airways are so small,' he explained calmly. 'Ella has picked up a nasty virus and it is affecting her breathing.'

The woman blanched and stared at the tiny figure on the trolley. 'But she's going to be OK?'

'We need to admit her to hospital,' Jack said, glancing up as the paediatrician walked into the room. 'This is Dr Armstrong, the paediatric registrar. He's going to take a look at her now and then we'll take her along to the ward.'

'Will I be able to stay with her?'

'Absolutely.' Jack nodded, his gaze reassuring. 'You can have a bed next to her cot.'

Deciding that Jack was never going to be able to extricate himself from the mother, Bryony briefed Dr Armstrong on the baby's condition.

She liked David Armstrong. He was warm and kind and he'd asked her out on several occasions.

And she'd refused of course. Because she always refused.

She *never* went on dates.

Bryony bit her lip, remembering Lizzie's letter to Santa. She wanted a daddy for Christmas. A pretty tall order for a woman who didn't date men, she thought dryly, picking up the baby's charts and handing them to David.

Dragging her mind back, she finished handing over and watched while David examined the baby himself.

A thoroughly nice man, she decided wistfully. So why couldn't she just accept his invitation to take their friendship a step further?

And then Jack strolled back to the trolley, tall,

broad-shouldered, confident and so shockingly hand-some that it made her gasp, and she remembered the reason why she didn't date men.

She didn't date men because she'd been in love with Jack since she'd been five years old. And apart from her one disastrous attempt to forget about him, which had resulted in Lizzie, she hadn't even *noticed* another man for her entire adult life.

Which just went to show how stupid she was, she reflected crossly, infuriated by her own stupidity.

Jack might be a brilliant doctor but he was also the most totally unsuitable man any woman could fall for. Women had affairs with Jack. They didn't fall in love with him. Not if they had any sense, because Jack had no intention of ever falling in love or settling down.

But, of course, she didn't have any sense.

It was fortunate that she'd got used to hiding the way she felt about him. He didn't have a clue that he'd featured in every daydream she'd had since she'd been a child. When other little girls had dreamed about faceless princes in fairy-tales, she'd dreamed about Jack. When her teenage friends had developed crushes on the boys at school, she'd still dreamed about Jack. And when she'd finally matured into a woman, she'd carried on dreaming about Jack.

Finally the baby was stable enough to be trans-ferred to the ward and Nicky pushed the trolley, ac-companied by the paediatric SHO, who had arrived to help, and the baby's mother.

Bryony started to tidy up Resus, ready for the next arrival, her mind elsewhere.

'Are you all right?' David Armstrong gave her a curious look. 'You're miles away.'

'Sorry.' She smiled. 'Just thinking.'

'Hard work, that, for a blonde,' Jack said mildly, and Bryony gave him a sunny smile, relaxed now that the baby was no longer her responsibility.

'Why are men like bank accounts?' she asked sweetly, ditching some papers in the bin. 'Because without a lot of money they don't generate much interest.'

David looked startled but Jack threw back his head and laughed.

'Then it's fortunate for me that I have a lot of money,' he said strolling across the room to her and looping her stethoscope back round her neck.

For a moment he stood there, looking down at her, his eyes laughing into hers as he kept hold of the ends of the stethoscope. Bryony looked back at him, hypnotised by the dark shadow visible on his hard jaw and the tiny muscle that worked in his cheek. He was so close she could almost touch him, but she'd never been allowed to do that.

Not properly.

He was her best friend.

They talked, they laughed and they spent huge amounts of time together. But they never crossed that line of friendship.

Jack's pager sounded and he let go of the stethoscope and reached into his pocket. 'Duty calls. If you're sure you can cope without me, I'll be off.'

'I'll struggle on,' Bryony said sarcastically, and he gave her that lazy wink that always reduced her legs to jelly.

'You do that. I'll see you later, then. Are you joining the team at the Drunken Fox tonight?'

'Yes. Mum's babysitting.'

The whole of the local mountain rescue team were
meeting for a drink to celebrate her brother's birthday.

'Good.' He gave a nod. 'See you there, then.'

And with that he strolled out of the room with his
usual easy confidence, letting the door swing closed
behind him.

David stared after him. 'Don't you mind the blonde
jokes and the fact that he calls you Blondie?'

Bryony shot him an amused look. 'He's called me
that for twenty-two years.' She fiddled with the
stethoscope that Jack had looped round her neck.
'He's just teasing.'

'You've known him for *twenty-two years*?'

'Amazing that I'm still sane, isn't it?' Bryony said
lightly. 'Jack was at school with my two brothers but
he spent more time in our house than his own.'
*Mainly because his parents had been going through
a particularly acrimonious divorce.*

'He's practically family. He and my brothers were
at medical school together.'

Nicky entered the room in time to hear that last
remark. 'I bet the three of them were lethal.'

'They certainly were.'

David looked at her in surprise. 'Of course—why
didn't I realise before? Tom Hunter, the consultant
obstetrician—he's your brother?'

Bryony smiled. 'That's right. And my other
brother, Oliver, is a GP. When I've finished my ro-
tation I'm going to join him in his practice. He's the
reason for the trip to the pub—it's his birthday today.'

Not that they needed an excuse for a trip to the pub. Most of the mountain rescue team members lived in the pub when they weren't working, training or on a callout.

David looked at her. 'I can't believe that I didn't click sooner that Tom Hunter is your brother.'

Bryony shrugged. 'Well, we don't know each other that well.'

'And whose fault is that?' David said in an undertone. 'I keep asking you out.'

And she kept refusing.

Conscious that Nicky was within earshot, Bryony handed David the last of the charts. 'Here you go. Everything you need on baby Ella. I hope she does OK.'

'Thanks.' He hesitated and then gave her a smile as he walked out of Resus.

'That man fancies you,' Nicky said dryly, and Bryony sighed.

'Yes, I know.'

'Don't tell me, you're in love with Jack, the same as every other woman on the planet.'

Bryony looked at her, carefully keeping her expression casual. She'd never admitted to *anyone* how she felt about Jack, and she wasn't going to start now. 'Jack's my best friend. I know him far too well to ever fall in love with him.'

'Then you're more sensible than the rest of the female population,' Nicky said happily. 'Every woman I know is in love with Jack Rothwell. He's rich, single and sexy as sin. And most of us could scratch your eyes out for being so close to him. According to rumour, he spends half his life hanging around your kitchen.'

Bryony smiled. When she'd lived at home Jack had always been there, and when she'd moved into her own cottage he'd taken to dropping round so often that he was almost part of the furniture. 'Don't get the wrong idea. Usually he's telling me about his latest girlfriend. He's my brothers' closest friend, he's my daughter's godfather and we've been in the mountain rescue team together for years. I can assure you there's nothing romantic about our relationship.'

Unfortunately.

Nicky sighed. 'Well, it sounds pretty good to me. I'd love to have him in my kitchen, if only for his decorative qualities. The guy is sublime.'

'Nicky, you're married.'

Nicky grinned. 'I know. But my hormones are still alive and kicking.'

Bryony busied herself restocking one of the equipment trays. Strictly speaking it wasn't her job but she didn't want to look at Nicky in case she gave herself away.

Her relationship with Jack was good.

They had a fantastic friendship.

But even the most fantastic friendship didn't soothe the ache in her heart.

She was about to say something else to Nicky when the doors to Resus opened again and one of the paramedics stuck his head round.

'Has the baby been transferred to the ward? Only I've got her father here.'

'I'll speak to him,' Bryony said immediately, glad

to be given an excuse to get away from the subject of Jack. She followed the paramedic out of the room.

A tall man in a suit was hovering anxiously in the corridor, his face white with strain.

'I'm Dr Hunter,' Bryony said, holding out her hand. 'I've been looking after Ella.'

'Oh, God…' he breathed out slowly, obviously trying to calm himself down. 'I came as soon as Pam called me but I was at a meeting in Penrith and the traffic was awful.'

Bryony gave an understanding smile and slowly outlined Ella's condition, careful to be realistic without painting too grim a picture.

'So she's on the ward?' He ran a hand over the back of his neck and gave a shuddering sigh. 'Sorry. I know I'm panicking like mad but she's my baby and—'

'It's OK,' Bryony said gently, putting a hand on his arm. 'You're her father and you're entitled to be worried.'

His shoulders sagged and he looked exhausted. 'You don't know what worry is until you have kids, do you?'

Bryony thought of Lizzie and shook her head. 'No,' she agreed softly, 'you certainly don't.'

'Do you have children yourself, Doctor?'

'I have a little girl.'

They shared a smile of mutual understanding. 'And the bond between a little girl and her daddy is so special, isn't it?'

Bryony tensed and then she smiled. 'It certainly is,' she croaked, feeling as though she'd been showered with cold water. 'Very special.'

She directed the man to the children's ward and stared after him, feeling sick inside.

She loved Lizzie so fiercely that she rarely thought about the fact that her little girl didn't have a father. She had plenty of father figures—her two brothers and Jack, and she'd always consoled herself that they were enough. But Lizzie obviously didn't think so or why would she have asked for a father for Christmas?

Lizzie wanted the real thing. She wanted a father to tuck her up at night. A father who would read to her and play with her. *A father who would panic and leave a meeting because she was sick.*

Bryony gave a groan and covered her face with her hands. How was she ever going to satisfy Lizzie's Christmas wish this year?

How was she going to produce a father when she didn't even date men and hadn't since Lizzie had been conceived? And not even then, really.

Bryony let her hands drop to her sides, torn with guilt at how selfish she'd been. Because of the way she felt about Jack, she'd shut men out of her life, never thinking about the long-term effect that would have on Lizzie.

It was true that she didn't want a man in her life, but it was also true that Lizzie needed and wanted a father.

And suddenly Bryony made a decision.

She was going to stop dreaming about Jack Rothwell. She was going to stop noticing his broad shoulders. She was going to stop noticing the way his cheeks creased when he smiled. She was going to stop thinking about what he looked like with his shirt off.

In fact, she was going to stop thinking about him altogether and start dating other men.

Finally she was going to get a life.

And Lizzie was going to get a daddy.

CHAPTER TWO

BRYONY paused outside the entrance to the pub, her breath clouding the freezing air. She could hear the muffled sounds of laughter and music coming from inside, and she lifted her chin and pushed open the door.

They were all there. The whole of the mountain rescue team, most of whom she'd known for years, crowding the bar and laughing together. In one corner of the bar a log fire crackled and the room was warm and welcoming.

'It's Blondie!'

There were good-natured catcalls from the moment they spotted her and Toby, the equipment officer, slipped off his stool and offered it to her with a flourish.

'Hi, guys.' She settled herself on the stool and smiled at the barman. 'Hi, Geoff. The usual, please.'

He reached for a bottle of grapefruit juice. 'On the hard stuff, Bryony?'

'That's me.' Bryony nodded her thanks and lifted the glass in a salute. 'Cheers, everyone. And happy birthday, Oliver.'

Her brother grinned. 'Thanks, babe. You OK?'

'I'm fine.' In fact, she was better than fine. She was brilliant. And she was finally going to restart her life.

As if to test that resolve, Jack strolled over to her and dropped a kiss on her cheek.

'What did the blonde say when she walked into the bar?'

'Ouch,' Bryony answered wearily, rolling her eyes in exasperation. 'And, Jack, you really need some new jokes. You're recycling them.'

He yawned. 'Well, I've been telling them for twenty-two years—what do you expect?'

'A bit of originality would be nice,' she said mildly, taking another sip of her drink and making a point of not looking at him. She wasn't going to notice Jack any more. There were plenty of men out there with good bodies. He wasn't the only one. 'Maybe I should dye my hair brown to help you out.'

'Brown? Don't you dare.' Jack's voice was husky and enticingly male. 'If you dyed your hair brown, you'd ruin all my jokes. We love you the way you are.'

Bryony took a gulp of her drink. He didn't love her. And he never would love her. Or, at least, not in the way she wanted him to love her.

'Bry, are you free on Thursday or Friday?' Oliver leaned across the bar and grabbed a handful of nuts. 'Mum wants to cook me a birthday dinner, whole family and Jack in attendance.'

Bryony put her glass down on the bar. 'Can't do Thursday.'

Jack frowned. 'You're on an early shift. Why can't you do it?'

Bryony hesitated. 'Because I have a date,' she said finally, and Oliver lifted his eyebrows.

'A date? You have *a date*?'

Jack's smile vanished like the sun behind a cloud. 'What do you mean, you have a date?' His voice was surprisingly frosty. 'Since when did you go on dates?'

Bryony took a deep breath and decided she may as well tell all. 'Since I saw Lizzie's Christmas list.'

At the mention of Lizzie, Jack's expression regained some of its warmth. 'She's made her list already?'

'She has indeed.'

'Don't tell me.' His voice was indulgent. 'She wants something pink. A new pair of pink wings for her fairy costume?'

'Nope.'

Oliver looked at her searchingly. 'Well? We're all dying to hear what she asked for. And what's it got to do with you going on a date?'

Bryony sat still for a moment, studying her empty glass. 'I'm going on a date,' she said slowly, 'because Lizzie wants a daddy.' She looked up and gave them a bland smile. 'Lizzie has asked for a daddy for Christmas.'

There was a long silence around the bar and the men exchanged looks.

It was Jack who eventually spoke first. 'Does she realise that they're not all they're cracked up to be?'

There was bitterness in his tone and Bryony frowned slightly. She knew that his parents had divorced when he'd been eight and she also knew that it had been a hideously painful experience for Jack.

But it was unlike him to ever mention it.

Like most men, Jack Rothwell didn't talk about his feelings.

'A *daddy*?' Oliver cleared his throat and exchanged looks with Tom. 'Does she have anyone in particular in mind?'

Bryony shook her head. 'No. She's leaving the choice up to Santa, but Mum gave me the letter and she's listed the qualities she's looking for.'

'She has?' Oliver gave an amazed laugh and glanced round at the others. 'And what are they?'

Bryony delved into her pocket and pulled out a rumpled piece of paper. She cleared her throat and started to read. 'I want a daddy who is strong so that he can swing me in the garden. I want a daddy who is funny and makes jokes. I want a daddy who lets me watch television before school and who won't make me eat sprouts because I hate them and I want a daddy who will meet me at the school gate and give me a hug like the other daddies sometimes do.' Bryony broke off at that point and swallowed hard, aware of the stunned silence around her. 'But most of all I want a daddy who will hug my mummy and stay with us for ever.'

No one spoke and Bryony gave a small shrug. 'That's it.'

She folded the paper carefully and put it back in her pocket, and Jack frowned.

'I never knew she wanted someone to pick her up from school,' he said gruffly, glancing between Oliver and Tom. 'We could do something about that, guys.'

'Sure,' Tom nodded agreement immediately and Bryony lifted a hand.

'Thank you, but no. That isn't what she wants. In fact, that would probably make it worse because the person who is picking her up isn't her daddy.'

Oliver frowned and rubbed a hand over the back of his neck. 'So where did it come from, this daddy business?'

'I don't know.' Bryony shrugged. 'I suppose she's just getting to that age where children notice differences between themselves and others. Most of the kids in her class are in traditional families.'

'You've been reading her too many fairy stories,' Jack said darkly, and she shrugged.

'She's a little girl, Jack. Little girls dream of weddings.'

Oliver grinned at Tom. 'Some big girls dream of weddings, too. I find it terrifying.'

'Stop it.' Bryony frowned in mock disapproval. 'How my daughter has ever grown up to be remotely normal with you three around her is a mystery to me. She's always asking me why none of you are married.'

'Did you tell her that we're too busy having fun?' Tom drawled, and Bryony rolled her eyes.

'Actually, I tell her that none of you have met the right woman yet, but that it's bound to happen soon.'

'Is it?' Oliver gave a shudder, his expression comical. 'I hope not.'

'You're awful. All three of you.'

Tom lifted an eyebrow in her direction. 'Well, you're not exactly an advert for relationships yourself, little sister. You haven't been on a date since Lizzie was born.'

'I know that. But that's all going to change.' Bryony lifted her chin. 'I've decided that Lizzie needs a daddy.'

'So what are you saying?' Jack was staring at her, all traces of humour gone from his handsome face. 'You're going to go out there and marry the first guy you meet just so that she can have a daddy?'

'Don't be ridiculous. Of course not.' Bryony lifted her chin and looked around her, her voice quiet but firm. 'I'm just saying that I'm going to start dating again.'

Oliver glanced at Tom and shrugged. 'Well, good for you.'

'Yeah.' Tom nodded and smiled at his sister. 'I think it's great. You've locked yourself up in a cupboard long enough. Get yourself out there, I say. Paint the town red. Or pink, if you're using Lizzie's colour scheme.'

Some of the other men in the team clapped her on the back and one or two made jokes about joining the queue to take her out.

Only Jack was silent, studying her with a brooding expression on his handsome face, his usual teasing smile notably absent. 'You really think you can find her a *daddy*?'

'I don't know.' Bryony gave a little shrug. 'Maybe not. But if I don't at least go on dates, it definitely won't happen.'

When he finally spoke his tone was chilly. 'So who's your date with on Thursday?'

Bryony looked at him in confusion, thinking that she'd never heard Jack use that tone before. He sounded...*angry*. But why would he be angry? The others actually seemed pleased for her. But not Jack.

'I'm not sure it's any of your business,' she teased him gently, trying to nudge their relationship back onto its usual platform, but on this occasion there was no answering smile.

'I'm Lizzie's godfather,' he reminded her, his blue eyes glittering in the firelight and a muscle working in his jaw. 'Who you choose as a *daddy* is very much my business.'

'You want to interview the guys I date, Jack?' She was still smiling, trying to keep it light, but he was glaring at her.

'Maybe.'

Bryony gave a disbelieving laugh, her own smile fading rapidly. 'You can't be serious.'

'You know absolutely nothing about the opposite sex, Blondie,' he said coldly. 'You've always refused to tell us who Lizzie's father was but he isn't around now which says quite a lot about your choice of men.'

Bryony gasped in shock. Lizzie's father wasn't a topic she discussed with anyone and Jack had never spoken to her like that before. He'd always been totally supportive of her status as a single mother.

'I don't know why you're looking so disapproving,' she said softly, aware that all the others had long since returned to their conversations and were no longer listening. Suddenly it was just the two of them and the tension in the atmosphere was increasing by the minute. 'You date all the time.'

His mouth tightened. 'I don't have a seven-year-old daughter.'

'But it's because of her that I'm doing this!'

Jack picked up his glass from the bar, a muscle flickering in his darkened jaw. 'That's ridiculous. You think you can just get out there and produce a happy family like magic?'

She sighed, knowing what was behind his words. 'No, I don't think that, Jack. But I think that it's time to see if I could maybe meet someone who seemed right for Lizzie and me.'

'Your life runs very smoothly,' he pointed out. 'Why complicate things?'

'Because Lizzie needs something more…' She hesitated. 'And I need something more, too, Jack. I've been on my own long enough.'

His mouth tightened. 'So basically you've suddenly decided to get out there and have fun.'

'And so what if I have?' Bryony looked at him, confused and exasperated. 'I just don't understand your attitude! You and my brothers have practically worked your way through most of the females in Cumbria.'

Streaks of colour touched his incredible cheekbones. 'That's different.'

Suddenly Bryony decided she'd had enough. 'Because you're a man and I'm a woman?'

'No.' His fingers tightened on his glass. 'Because I don't have any responsibilities.'

'No. You've made sure of that. And there's no need to remind me of my responsibilities to Lizzie. That's what started this, remember?' She glared at him, suddenly angry with him for being so judgmental. 'Lizzie wants a daddy and it's my job to find her one. And

I'm more than happy to try and find someone I can live with because frankly I'm sick and tired of being on my own, too.'

How could she have been so stupid as to put herself on ice for so long? She should have realised just how deep-rooted his fear of commitment was. Should have realised that Jack Rothwell would never settle down with anyone, let alone her.

It was definitely time to move on.

'I'm going home,' she said coldly, slipping off the barstool and avoiding his gaze. 'I'll see you at work tomorrow.'

She heard his sharp intake of breath and knew that he was going to try and stop her, but she virtually ran to the door, giving him no opportunity to intercept her.

She didn't want to talk to him. Didn't want to hear all the reasons why she shouldn't have a boyfriend when he dated a non-stop string of beautiful women.

She'd call Oliver later and apologise for ducking out without saying goodbye, but she knew he wouldn't mind. They were a close family and she adored her brothers. At least they'd been encouraging.

Which was more than could be said for Jack.

Why had he acted like that? All right, he was absolutely against marriage, but it wasn't *his* marriage they were talking about. It was *hers*, and Jack was usually warm and supportive of everything she did. They *never* argued. They were best friends.

She unlocked her car quickly, feeling tears prick her eyes.

Well, if dating other men meant losing Jack as a

friend, then so be it. She'd wasted enough time on him. He didn't even notice her, for goodness' sake!

And if she'd needed confirmation that it was time to move on, she had it now.

Jack banged his empty glass down on the bar and cursed under his breath.

'Nice one, Jack,' Oliver said mildly, clapping him on the shoulder and glancing towards the door. 'I thought the three of us agreed that we weren't going to bring up the thorny subject of Lizzie's father.'

Jack groaned and ran a hand over his face. 'I know, I know.' He let out a long breath. 'It's just that she knows *nothing* about men—'

'She's twenty-seven.'

'So?' Jack glared at Oliver. 'And we know that she hasn't been out with a man since Lizzie was conceived. That guy broke her heart! I don't want her making the same mistake again. She's obviously never got over him. What if she picks someone on the rebound?'

Tom joined them. 'I'm not sure you can rebound after seven years,' he said mildly, and Jack's mouth tightened.

'So why does Lizzie never date, then?'

Tom looked at him steadily. 'I don't know...'

'Yes you do.' Jack's eyes narrowed as he studied his friend. 'You think you know. I can tell.'

Tom shook his head and drained his glass. 'No. I don't know.' He studied his empty glass. 'But I can guess.'

Jack frowned. 'So what's your guess?'

Tom gave a funny smile and looked at Oliver. 'My guess is that she has a particular guy on her mind,' he drawled casually, 'and until she gets over him, she can't move on.'

'Precisely what I said,' Jack said smugly. 'She needs to get over Lizzie's father.'

And with that he grabbed his jacket and strode out of the pub after her.

Oliver looked at Tom. 'I always thought he was a bright guy. How did he ever come top in all those exams?'

Tom gave a faint smile. 'He'll get there in the end.'

'Unless Bry meets someone else.'

'Bryony has been in love with Jack for twenty-two years,' Tom said calmly, glancing at the barman and waggling his glass. 'She's never going to fall in love with anyone else.'

'So what happens now?'

Tom reached for his wallet. 'I think we're in for a very interesting few weeks. Happy birthday, bro. This one's on me.'

Damn.

Jack strode out to the car park, cursing himself for being so tactless. He couldn't believe he'd argued with Bryony. He *never* argued with Bryony. Or, at least, not seriously. Bryony was the nearest he had to family and their relationship was all banter and teasing and a great deal of confiding. Well, on his part at least. He told her everything about his relationships and she was always giving him little suggestions. And that was one of the things he loved about their friendship. Unlike the women he dated, Bryony never tried to change him or lecture him. She just accepted him as he was. He was more comfortable in her kitchen than any other place in the world. And now he'd upset her.

What the hell had come over him?

He looked round the car park, part of him hoping that she was still there, but of course she was long gone. He just hoped she wasn't driving too quickly. The air was freezing and the roads would be icy.

He gritted his teeth and swore under his breath. She'd been really upset by his comments and there was a very strong chance that he'd made her cry. Despite the fact that she rarely let him see it, he knew she was soft-hearted. He'd known her since she was five, for goodness' sake, and he knew her better than anyone.

Realising that he had a big apology to make, he ran a hand over his face and strolled to his car, pressing the remote control on his keyring.

He could drive over to her cottage now, of course, but she'd still be mad with him and anyway her mother would be there so they wouldn't be able to talk properly.

No. The apology was best left until they could be alone.

If he'd been dating her he would have sent her flowers, but he'd never sent Bryony flowers in his life, and if he did she'd think he'd gone mad.

He slid into his sports car and dropped his head back against the seat.

No doubt, now that word was out that she was going to start dating, flowers would be arriving for her thick and fast.

He growled low in his throat, tension rising in him as he contemplated the impact that her announcement had made.

Why had she chosen to tell the whole pub? Didn't she know that all the guys lusted after her? That with her long silken blonde hair and her fabulous curvy body, she couldn't walk across a room without stopping conversations? And he felt every bit as protective towards her as he knew her brothers did.

And now some sleazy guy would come along and take advantage of her, and she was so trusting and inexperienced with men she wouldn't even notice until it was too late.

Jack reversed the car out of its space, crunching the gears viciously. Well, *not* while he was available to prevent it happening.

She'd become pregnant in her second year at medical school and neither he nor her brothers had been around to sort the guy out. Damn it, she hadn't even told them who he was. Just mumbled something about the whole thing being a mistake and refused to even discuss it even though Tom and Oliver had pumped her for hours.

Well, there wasn't going to be another mistake, Jack thought grimly, his strong hands tightening on the wheel. Because now there was Lizzie's happiness to think of, too. No one was going to hurt either one of his girls.

From now on, if any guy so much as *looked* at

Bryony the wrong way, if there was even a *scent* of someone messing her around, he'd step in and floor them.

Satisfied that he was back in control of the situation, he stopped trying to pulverise his precious car and slowed his pace.

All he needed to do now was plan. He needed to know exactly whom she was dating so that he could issue a warning.

Bryony let herself into the house and found her mother in the kitchen. 'Is she asleep?'

'Fast asleep.' Her mother dried her hands on a towel. 'You're back early, darling. Is something wrong?'

'No.' Bryony unwrapped the scarf from around her neck and tossed it onto the chair. Her coat followed.

'Bryony, I'm your mother. I can tell when something is wrong.'

Bryony glared at her, her eyes sparkling with unshed tears. 'Jack Rothwell, that's what's wrong!'

'Ah.' Her mother gave a smile and turned to put the kettle on. 'Tea?'

'I suppose so.' Bryony slumped into the nearest chair and sighed. 'He is the most infuriating man.'

'Is he?'

'You know he is.'

Her mother reached for the tea bags. 'I know that you two have been very close for almost the whole of your lives,' she said mildly. 'I'm sure that whatever it is you've quarrelled about will go away.'

'The man dates every woman on the planet,' Bryony said, still outraged by his attitude, 'but when

I announce that I'm going to start going out with men, he's suddenly disapproving. And he had the nerve to lecture me on my responsibilities to Lizzie!'

'Did he?' Her mother looked thoughtful. 'That's very interesting.'

'Interesting?' Bryony shot her mother an incredulous look. 'Irritating, you mean. And hypocritical. How many girlfriends has Jack Rothwell had since I first met him?'

Her mother poured the tea. 'Quite a few, I should think.'

'Half the planet,' Bryony said flatly. 'He certainly isn't in a position to lecture me about morals.'

'I imagine he thought he was protecting Lizzie.'

Bryony stared at her. 'From what?'

Her mother put two mugs on the table and sat down opposite her. 'Jack hasn't had a very positive experience of marriage, sweetheart.'

'You mean because of his parents?'

Her mother's mouth tightened with disapproval. 'Well, you know my opinion on that. They were grown-ups. He was a child. They should have sorted out their differences amicably. After his father walked out, Jack spent most of his childhood at our house and I don't think his mother even noticed he wasn't at home. She was too busy enjoying herself to remember that she had a child.'

Bryony bit her lip, suddenly realising why Jack might have been so sensitive about her dating. 'But I wouldn't do that. That isn't what this is about.'

'I know. But you understand Jack better than anyone,' her mother said calmly. 'He wasn't thinking about you, darling. He was thinking about his own experiences.'

Bryony bit her lip. 'Do you think I should start dating, Mum?'

'Certainly I think you should date,' her mother replied calmly. 'I've always thought you should date, but you've always been too crazy about Jack to notice anyone else.'

Bryony stared at her, opened her mouth to deny it and then caught the look in her mother's eye and closed it again. 'You know that?'

'I'm your mother. Of course I know that.'

'He doesn't notice me.'

'You're a huge part of Jack's life,' her mother said mildly. 'He virtually lives here. But that's going to have to change if you really are going to date other men.'

Bryony curled her hands round her mug. 'But I don't want it to change my friendship with Jack.'

'One day you'll get married again,' her mother said quietly, 'and I can't see any man wanting to see Jack lounging in your kitchen every time he comes home from work. Of course your friendship is going to change.'

Bryony stared into her mug, a hollow feeling inside her. She didn't want things to change. Despite their row, she couldn't imagine not having Jack in her life.

But she couldn't carry on the way she was now, for Lizzie's sake.

'Then I suppose I'll just have to get used to that,' she said, raising her mug in the air. 'Cheers. To my future.'

Her mother lifted her mug in response. 'May it turn out the way you want it to,' she said cryptically, and Bryony let out a long breath.

She wasn't really sure what *she* wanted.

But she knew Lizzie needed a daddy.

The next morning she was woken by her pager.

'Is that a callout?' Lizzie was by her bed in a flash, her eyes huge. 'Is someone in trouble on the mountain?'

Bryony picked up her pager and was reading the message when the phone rang. Lizzie grabbed it immediately.

'Hunter household, Elizabeth Hunter speaking,' she said formally, the angle of her chin suggesting that she was very proud of herself. She listened for a moment and then a smile spread across her face. 'Hello, Jack! Yes, Mummy's right here… I'll tell her. Will I see you later?'

Bryony pulled on her clothes and sprinted to the bathroom to clean her teeth. By the time she'd finished, Lizzie was off the phone.

'There's a party of Duke of Edinburgh Award boys overdue,' she said importantly. 'They're sending out the whole team but Sean wants you and Jack to be an advance party. Jack is picking you up in five minutes.'

'Five minutes.' Bryony hurried through to the kitchen, grabbed an apple from the fruit bowl and dropped some bread in the toaster. 'Get your school things, sweetheart. Jack and I will drop you at

Grandma's on the way past and she can take you to school.'

Lizzie sprinted off and Bryony sent up a silent prayer of thanks that she had her mother close by. How did single parents manage without mothers?

By the time Jack hammered on the door, Lizzie was dressed and was standing by the door with her school-bag, munching toast.

She stood on tiptoe and opened the door.

'Hi, there.' Jack stooped and swung her into his arms, squeezing her tightly. 'Are we dropping you with Grandma?'

'We certainly are.' Bryony walked into the hall and picked up her rucksack and the other bits and pieces that she'd piled by the door, avoiding Jack's gaze. She was grateful that Lizzie was there. At least it prevented her from having to continue the conversation from the night before.

She was still hurt and angry by Jack's response to her announcement that she was going to start dating.

They piled into the mountain rescue vehicle and Jack drove down the lane that led to Bryony's cottage and turned onto the main road.

'So what's the story?' Bryony twisted her blonde hair into a ponytail and pushed it under a woolly hat. Then she rummaged in her bag for her gloves.

Jack kept his eyes on the road. 'Two boys have been reported overdue. They should have been back down last night but they didn't appear.'

Bryony frowned. 'So why did no one call the team last night?'

'They were camping and didn't leave their plans

with anyone so no one noticed until their friends stumbled into camp this morning and raised the alarm. The weather was foul last night, which is doubtless why Sean is worried.'

Lizzie stared at him, her eyes huge. 'Have they called the helicopter?'

'Yes, sweetheart.' Jack glanced at her with a smile. 'But the weather is pretty awful so Sean, the MRT leader, wants your mum and me to get going up that mountain in case we can help.'

'Why do you and Mummy always go together?'

Jack turned his attention back to the road and pulled the vehicle up outside Bryony's mother's house. 'Because your mum and I have always worked together in the mountain rescue team,' he said lightly. 'When your mum trained, I was her buddy. I looked after her.'

'And you still look after her,' Lizzie said happily, jumping down from the vehicle and grabbing her school-bag.

'I don't need looking after,' Bryony said crossly, glaring at Jack and calling after Lizzie, 'Sweetheart, ask Grandma to give you some more breakfast. I'll see you later.'

They waited until Bryony's mother opened the door and then Jack gave a wave and hit the accelerator.

Suddenly Bryony was very aware that it was just the two of them and she stared out of the window, for the first time in her life not knowing what to say.

'We think we know where they are,' Jack told her, flicking the indicator and turning down a narrow road.

'It's just a question of what state they'll be in when we get there.'

Which was why Sean had sent them as the advance party, Bryony thought. He wanted doctors. Which meant that he was anticipating trouble.

She picked up the map. 'What's the grid reference?'

He told her and she traced it with her finger. 'They're in the ghyll?'

'Sounds like it.'

Bryony looked at him in concern. 'But the water level is terribly high after all that rain we've had…'

'That's right.' Jack's voice was even and he brought the vehicle to a halt. 'Which is why we need to get a move on. Personally I doubt they'll be able to fly a helicopter in this. Sean has called the whole team out, but we're going on ahead.'

He sprang out of the vehicle and reached for the equipment that they'd need. They worked quickly and quietly, each knowing what the other was doing.

'You ready?' Jack lifted an eyebrow in her direction and she nodded.

'Let's go.'

Jack set off at a fast pace and Bryony followed, knowing that speed was important. After a night out in the open in the wet and temperatures below freezing, the boys would be in serious trouble.

They had to reach them fast.

The path grew steeper, the mist came down and Jack shook his head. 'It's November, it's freezing cold and the visibility is zero.' He hitched his rucksack more comfortably on his broad shoulders and squinted into the mist. 'Who the hell chooses to climb mountains at this time of year?'

'You do it all the time,' Bryony pointed out, checking her compass again. 'One of these days we're going to be out here rescuing you.'

'Never.' He winked and gave her a sexy grin. 'I am invincible.'

Bryony rolled her eyes. 'And arrogant.' She stopped dead and he looked at her questioningly.

'Why have you stopped?'

'Because your ego is blocking my path.'

Jack laughed and then the laughter faded. 'Listen, Blondie, about last night—'

'Not now,' Bryony said hastily. She really didn't want to tackle the subject again so soon, especially not halfway up a mountain.

'I just wanted to apologise,' he said softly. 'I was out of line. You're a brilliant mother and I know you'll do what's right for Lizzie.'

Stunned by his apology, Bryony lost her ability to speak. She'd never heard Jack apologise for anything before.

'Let's forget it,' she mumbled, and Jack nodded, his blue eyes studying her closely.

'All right. We'll talk about it later.' He glanced up the path and frowned. 'There is no way that helicopter is going to fly in this.'

'So we evacuate them down the mountain.'

He nodded and then turned to her, his eyes twinkling wickedly. 'Why did the blonde stare at the can of frozen orange juice?' He leaned forward and tucked a strand of hair back under her hat. 'Because it said ''concentrate''.'

Bryony tipped her head on one side and stared back at him. 'Why are men like government bonds?' He lifted an eyebrow, his eyes dancing, and she smiled sweetly. 'Because they take for ever to mature. Now, can we get on with this rescue?'

They stuck to the path and the mist grew thicker. Jack's radio crackled to life and he paused and had a quick conversation with Sean back at base.

'They're sending out the whole team,' he told her when he came off the radio, 'but I reckon we must be nearly at the place where they were last seen.'

Bryony stood still, listening, but all she could hear was the rush of water. The freezing air snaked through her clothing and she shivered.

'If they didn't have any protection last night, they won't have stood a chance,' she muttered, and Jack nodded, his handsome face serious.

'Better find them, fast.'

He started up the track again and then stopped, squinting down into the ghyll. 'Do you see something?'

'What?' Bryony stepped towards the edge but Jack reached out a strong arm and clamped her against him.

'If it's all the same to you, I'd rather you didn't go over the edge, too,' he said dryly, keeping his arm round her as he peered through the mist into the ghyll again.

Bryony held her breath, painfully conscious of his hard body pressed against hers.

'I don't see anything.' She wondered when he was going to let her go and was about to ask when she spotted a flash of red below them. 'OK, I see something.'

'Me, too.' Jack released her. 'There's a path here but it's narrow and slippery. Think you can manage, Blondie? You have to put one leg in front of the other and not fall over.'

'It'll be a struggle, but I'll do my best,' Bryony assured him earnestly, relieved that their relationship seemed to have restored itself to its usual level. 'What about you? Think you can find your way without asking for directions?'

They kept up the banter as they picked their way down the path, and finally they reached the bottom and immediately saw the boys huddled together by a boulder.

Jack closed the distance in seconds and dropped to his haunches, his expression concerned. 'Hi, there— nice day for a stroll in the mountains.'

'We thought no one was ever coming,' the boy whispered, his teeth chattering as he spoke. 'Martyn keeps falling asleep and leaving me on my own.'

'Right. Put a bivouac tent over them.' Jerking his head to indicate that Bryony should deal with the conscious child, Jack shifted his position so that he could examine the other boy.

He was lying still, moaning quietly, his cheeks pale and his lips blue.

Jack spoke to him quietly and checked his pulse while Bryony checked the other boy for injuries. Once she was satisfied that he was just cold and shaken, she erected the tent and helped him to scramble inside a casualty bag.

'What's your name?'

'Sam.'

'Well, Sam, that will keep you warm until we can get you off this mountain,' she assured him, and he gave a little sob.

'Martyn fell. His leg is awful. I saw bone.'

Bryony slipped an arm round him and gave him a hug. 'Don't you worry about that now,' she said softly. 'We'll sort him out and get you both home. I'm going to pour you a hot drink and that will warm you up.'

She grabbed the flask that she'd packed and poured thick creamy chocolate into a mug.

'Here—drink this. I'll be back in a sec.' Aware that Jack was going to need her help, she slid out of the tent and moved over to him.

'Sam says that his friend fell.'

Jack nodded, still checking the child over. 'He's got a compound fracture of his tib and fib and he's bleeding a lot. We need to get a line in, Blondie, and then splint that leg.'

Bryony reached for the rucksack and found what they needed, aware that Jack was on the radio again, updating Sean on their position and the condition of the boys.

By the time he'd finished on the radio Bryony had a line in. 'Do you want to give him fluid?'

Jack nodded. 'And then we need to splint that leg. It will help the pain and reduce blood loss.' He leaned over the boy, talking quietly, explaining what they were doing, and Bryony gave a sigh. He was so good when anyone was in trouble. A rock. And he always knew what to do. Her confidence came from being with him.

She covered the wound on the leg with a sterile saline-soaked dressing while Jack carefully removed the boy's boot.

He placed his fingers on Martyn's foot, feeling for a pulse. 'That's fine—let's splint this leg. We're just going to give you something for the pain, Martyn, and then we're going to put your leg in a splint. Then we're going to warm you up and get you off this mountain.'

Bryony gave a shiver. The temperature was dropping fast and even in her top-quality gear she could feel the cold.

By the time they'd splinted the boy's leg, Sean had arrived with the rest of the mountain rescue team.

'Nice day for a walk,' he drawled, glancing around him at the thick mist. 'The views are fantastic.'

Bryony smiled. 'Absolutely fantastic,' she said sarcastically. 'Enjoy your stroll, did you?'

Sean grinned in appreciation. 'Didn't want to rush things,' he said, lifting an eyebrow in Jack's direction. 'Well?'

'We need a helicopter but I don't suppose there's any chance of that.'

'You suppose correctly.'

Jack sighed and checked the pulses on the boy's foot again. 'So we'd better carry them off, then. Good. I needed a workout.'

It seemed to take ages to organise both boys onto

stretchers but eventually they managed to carry them
out of the ghyll and started down the mountain.

By the time they reached the valley floor the mist
had cleared and it was a sunny day.

'I don't believe this,' Bryony muttered, tugging off
her hat and shaking her hair loose. 'What is it with
our weather?'

Both boys were loaded into the mountain rescue
team ambulance and then transferred to hospital under
Sean's supervision while Jack and Bryony followed
behind.

'Are you working today?' Jack glanced across at
her and she nodded.

'Yes. I'm on a late. Why?'

He returned his attention to the road. 'I thought you
had a date.'

Bryony looked at him warily. 'That's tomorrow,
but I don't know if I'm going because Mum has to
go and visit someone in Kendal so I don't think she
can babysit.'

'I'll babysit for you.'

Bryony stared at him. 'You?'

'Why not?' His eyes were fixed on the road. 'I
often babysit for you. It gives me a chance to talk to
my godchild. I like it.'

Bryony looked at him suspiciously. 'But last
night…' She broke off and bit her lip, not really wanting to bring the subject up in case it rocked the peace
that had resumed between them. 'Last night you said
that you didn't think I should be dating.'

'And I've already apologised for that,' he said,
flicking the indicator and turning into the road that

led to the hospital. 'And to make up for it, I'll babysit for you. What time do you want me?'

Still feeling uneasy about the whole thing but not knowing why, Bryony gave a shrug. 'Seven-thirty?'

'Seven-thirty is perfect. There's just one thing...' He pulled up in the ambulance bay and yanked on the handbrake. 'You haven't told me who you're going out with.'

There was something in his smooth tones that made her glance at him warily but his handsome face was impassive.

She paused with her hand on the door. 'David.'

'David Armstrong? The paediatrician?' Jack's expression didn't change but she sensed something that made her uneasy.

'Look, Jack—'

'I'll be there at seven-thirty. Now, let's get on. I need to get antibiotics into Martyn and call the surgeons. That wound is going to need some attention.'

And with that he sprang out of the vehicle, leaving her staring after him.

Jack was going to babysit while she went on a date?

It seemed harmless enough, generous even, so why did she have such a strong feeling that something wasn't quite right?

CHAPTER THREE

'MUMMY, you look pretty.'

'Do you think so?' Bryony surveyed her reflection in the mirror, wondering whether the dress was right for the evening that David had in mind. He'd said dinner in a smart restaurant, but she never went to smart restaurants so she wasn't that sure what to wear.

In the end she'd settled for the little black dress that her mother had given her three Christmases ago and which she'd never worn.

She'd fastened her hair on top of her head, found a pair of pretty, dangly earrings and dabbed perfume over her body.

And she had to admit that she was looking forward to going out with a man.

So much so that when the doorbell rang she opened the door with a wide smile.

'Hi, Jack.' Her face glowed and she stood to one side to let him in. 'There's a casserole in the oven. I assumed you wouldn't have eaten—'

'I haven't eaten.' His eyes slid down her body and he frowned, his expression suddenly hostile.

Bryony felt the confidence ooze out of her. She'd thought that she looked good but, judging from the look on Jack's face, she obviously didn't.

'Come through to the kitchen,' she said quickly, suddenly wishing that she'd worn something different. Obviously the black dress didn't suit her. 'We've got time for a quick drink before David gets here. He was held up in clinic.'

Jack's mouth tightened with disapproval. 'So he's going to be late, then.'

'Well, only because a child with asthma was admitted at the last minute,' Bryony said mildly, tugging open the fridge and reaching for a bottle of wine. 'You know how it is.'

'Do I?'

Instead of settling himself at her kitchen table as he usually did, he prowled round the room, his eyes constantly flickering back to her dress.

Trying to ignore his intense scrutiny, Bryony poured two glasses of wine and handed him one. 'Here you are. Cheers.'

He took the wine and put it on the table, his eyes fixed on her legs.

Bryony felt her whole body warm with embarrassment. She hardly ever showed her legs. She usually wore trousers for work because they were more practical, and when she went to the pub with the rest of the mountain rescue team she wore trousers, too.

But tonight, for the first time in ages, she'd put on a pair of sheer, black stockings and she was beginning to wish she hadn't.

'You hate it, don't you?' she croaked, and his eyes lifted and welded to hers.

'Hate what?'

She swallowed. 'The way I look. My dress. Me. You're staring and staring.'

Jack let out a breath. 'That's because I don't think you should be going out with a man dressed like that,' he said tightly. 'It sends out all the wrong messages.'

She frowned at him, totally confused. 'What messages?'

He tensed. 'Well—that you're available.'

'Jack,' she said patiently, 'I *am* available. That is the message I want to send out.'

'So you wear a skirt that's up to your bottom?' He glared at her and she stared back helplessly, totally confused by his attitude.

She'd met some of the girls that he'd dated and they were almost all blondes with skirts up round their bottoms.

'Jack, my skirt is just above the knee,' she pointed out, glancing down at herself to check that half her dress hadn't fallen off without her knowledge. 'It is nowhere near my bottom.'

'Well, it's definitely too low in the front,' he said hoarsely, reaching across the kitchen table, yanking a flower out of a vase and snapping it halfway up the stem. 'Try this.'

He walked up to her and slipped the flower down the neckline of her dress and stood back with a frown.

'That's a bit better.'

'Jack—'

Before she could say anything, Lizzie came running into the room wearing a pink gauze fairy dress and wearing wings. 'Jack, Jack!' She flung herself into his arms and he picked her up and gave her a kiss on the cheek.

'Hello, beautiful. Shouldn't you be in bed?'

'I was waiting for you.' Lizzie curled her legs round his waist and waggled her finger at him. 'Look. I'm wearing three rings. They're sweets really, but aren't they great?'

Jack dutifully studied her finger. 'Really great. And if you get hungry in the night you can eat them.'

Lizzie beamed. 'Can we play a game, Jack?'

'Sure.' Jack put her down gently and smiled indulgently. 'Any game you like. Just name it.'

'Weddings.'

Jack's smile vanished. *'Weddings?'*

Lizzie nodded happily. 'Yes, you know. You're the boy and I'm the girl and we get married.'

Jack gave a shudder. 'I don't know the rules, sweetheart.'

Bryony covered her hand with her mouth to hide her smile. Jack was brilliant at playing with her daughter but 'Weddings' was the one game guaranteed to bring him out in a rash.

'It's easy,' Lizzie assured him happily. 'We hold hands and then we get married.'

Jack ran a hand over the back of his neck and looked at Bryony for help, but she simply smiled.

'Weddings, Jack,' she said softly, her eyes dancing as she looked at him. 'That well-known game enjoyed by men and women the world over.'

His eyes shot daggers at her but he turned to Lizzie with a resigned sigh. 'All right, peanut, tell me what I have to do.'

'Well, first I have to go and dress up.' Lizzie shot out of the room and Jack turned on Bryony.

'She's playing *weddings*?'

'She's a girl, Jack,' Bryony said mildly. 'Girls play weddings.'

'I'm breaking out in a sweat here,' he muttered dryly, and she grinned unsympathetically.

'She's seven years old. I think you can cope. Great practice for when you do the real thing.'

His gaze locked on hers, his blue eyes mocking. 'You know I'm never doing the real thing.'

'Well, don't tell my daughter that. I don't want her saddled with your prejudices about relationships.'

'I should be teaching her about reality.'

Before Bryony could answer, Lizzie danced back into the room, this time wearing a full-length sparkly dress complete with glittering tiara.

Jack blinked. 'Wow...' He cleared his throat. 'I didn't know you had a tiara.'

'I've got seven,' Lizzie said proudly, and Bryony smiled cheerfully.

'A girl can never have too many tiaras, can she, Lizzie?'

'Come on, Jack.' Lizzie grabbed his hand. 'First we have to hold hands and walk across the carpet. Mummy can video us.'

Jack glanced at Bryony who could barely stand up she was laughing so much. 'Great idea, Lizzie,' she choked. 'It would make great viewing at the MRT Christmas party. Jack finally getting married.'

Jack scowled, but his eyes were dancing. 'Revenge is going to be sweet, Blondie,' he warned softly, but he was laughing too and shaking his head as Lizzie dragged him into the sitting room and Bryony reached for the video camera.

To give him his due, Jack treated the whole occasion with the appropriate amount of solemnity, sweeping Lizzie's hand to his lips as if she were a princess.

At first Bryony was laughing so much that she

could hardly keep the camera steady, but as she watched Jack playing his role to perfection and saw the delight on her little girl's face, her smile faded and she felt an ache growing inside her. Jack was so brilliant with Lizzie. And although he couldn't see it himself, he'd make a wonderful father.

She was reminding herself firmly that she wasn't going to think that way any more when the doorbell rang and she realised that her date had arrived.

She answered the door and David stood on the doorstep, flourishing a bunch of flowers.

'Are they for me? They're beautiful, thank you.' She smiled at him and was wondering whether she ought to kiss him when she heard Jack clear his throat behind her.

'You'll need a coat, Blondie,' he said coolly, the humour gone from his eyes as he held out the long woollen coat that she always wore to work and which covered her from her neck to her ankles.

'I was going to take my pashmina,' Bryony began, but Jack walked up behind her and draped the coat over her shoulders, pulling it closed at the front so that not one single inch of her was visible.

'It's too cold for a pashmina,' he grated. 'You don't want to get hypothermia over dinner.' He stood back and gave David a nod. 'She needs to be home at eleven.'

'What?' Bryony gaped at him and then gave an embarrassed laugh. They hadn't even discussed what time he wanted her home but she'd assumed that she could be as late as she liked. She knew Jack well enough to know that he didn't go to bed early himself.

And invariably he slept in her spare room. So why was he saying that she needed to be in by eleven?

David gave an awkward smile. 'Eleven is fine.'

Bryony scowled, less than impressed that he hadn't stood up to Jack. Surely he should have said that he'd bring her home when he was ready, or some such thing. She knew for sure that if someone had told Jack that he should bring a girl home by eleven he would have kept her out for the whole night just to prove a point.

But she'd promised herself that she wasn't going to think about Jack, she reminded herself hastily, taking the flowers through to the kitchen and putting them in water.

When she arrived back at the door the two men were staring at each other. David looked mildly embarrassed and Jack was standing, feet planted firmly apart, very much the dominant male and not in the slightest bit embarrassed.

Deciding that Jack had definitely gone mad, Bryony held out a hand to David and smiled. 'Shall we go?'

'Jack.' Lizzie tugged his arm and frowned at him. 'You're skipping bits.'

Jack shook himself and stared down at the book he was supposed to be reading. 'Am I?'

'Yes.' Lizzie grabbed the book from him and went back two pages. 'You didn't read this page at all. And you've got a funny look on your face.'

'Have I?'

Jack tried to concentrate on the pink fairy flying across the page of the book but all he could see was

Bryony in that dress. He hadn't seen her legs since she'd been in the netball team at school and he and her brothers had gone to matches to cheer her on, but he now realised that his best friend had sensational legs.

And if she was going to start showing them, how the hell was he going to protect her?

And it wasn't just her legs, of course…

He closed his eyes, trying to forget the shadowy dip between her full breasts revealed by the cut of her dress.

Right now they were in the restaurant and David was probably sitting opposite her, staring into paradise.

With a soft curse he stood up and the book fell to the floor.

'You said a rude word, Jack,' Lizzie said mildly, leaning over and retrieving the book.

'Sorry.' Suddenly seized by inspiration, he gave Lizzie a smile. 'How would you like to call your mother and say goodnight?'

'Now?'

'Sure, why not?' Before Dr Armstrong had time to get too hot and over-eager. Suddenly driven by an urgency that he couldn't explain, Jack grabbed Lizzie's hand and dragged her into the kitchen. 'We'll ring her mobile.'

Lizzie looked at him uncertainly. 'Grandma says we only ring if there's an emergency.'

Jack was already pressing the keys. 'Trust me, this is an emergency,' he assured her, his mind still mentally on Bryony's creamy breasts. His mouth tightened. 'A big emergency. Her baby girl wants to say goodnight.'

Trying to ignore the fact that Lizzie was looking at him as though he was slightly mad, Jack held the receiver and waited for Bryony to answer.

As the phone rang and rang, his heart started to thud in his chest.

Why the hell wasn't she answering?

Unless she wasn't at dinner after all. What if the rat had taken one look at that dress and whisked Bryony back to his flat?

'Uncle Jack, you're breathing really fast,' Lizzie said, climbing onto a kitchen stool, her fairy wings still attached to her back. 'And you look weird.'

He felt weird.

Why wasn't she answering?

David sat back in his chair. 'Is that your phone?'

Bryony looked at him, startled, and then picked up her bag. 'Oh, my goodness, yes.' She fumbled in her handbag, her stomach turning over. 'I hope nothing is wrong with Lizzie. I don't usually get phoned…'

She delved amongst tissues, make-up, notebooks and various pink hairbands that belonged to her daughter and eventually found the phone.

Feeling distinctly nervous, she answered it. 'Jack?' She cast an apologetic look at David. 'Is something wrong?'

She listened for a moment and then frowned. 'I'm in the restaurant, Jack. Where did you think I was? Well, I couldn't find my phone.'

At that moment the waiter delivered their starter and Bryony smiled her thanks, trying to ignore his look of disapproval. She knew that mobile phones were banned from lots of restaurants but she refused to turn hers off in case Lizzie needed her.

But it seemed that all Lizzie wanted was to say goodnight. Strange, Bryony thought as she spoke to her daughter and then ended the call. Lizzie was normally fine. Especially when she was with Jack. She loved being with Jack.

'Everything OK?' David looked at her quizzically and she smiled.

'Fine. Sorry about that.'

She picked up her fork and tucked into her starter, determined to relax. Part of her mind was still dwelling on the fact that Jack had hated her dress, but she ignored it. David seemed to think she looked nice and that was all that mattered.

They chattered about work and the mountain rescue team and they were just tucking into their main course when her phone rang again.

This time Bryony heard it immediately and stopped the ringing before the waiter had time to glare at her.

It was Jack again, this time telling her that Lizzie was refusing to take her fairy wings off.

Bryony frowned. This was a guy who could save a life halfway up a mountain in a howling gale with nothing more than a penknife and a piece of string.

And he was calling her about *fairy wings*?

'Just take them off when she's asleep, Jack,' she muttered, smiling apologetically at David as she slipped the phone back into her bag.

She tried valiantly to resume the conversation but when Jack called for the third time, David raised his hand and gestured to the waiter.

'I think I'll take you home,' he said dryly. 'Then you can answer Jack's questions in person and he won't have to keep calling you.'

'Sorry.' Bryony blushed slightly. As a first date it had been less than perfect. 'I honestly don't know what's the matter with him. He and Lizzie are normally fine together.'

David drove her home and then walked her up the path to her cottage. At the front door he paused, his expression thoughtful as he looked down at her.

Bryony stared back, feeling slightly awkward. Was he going to kiss her?

Suddenly she felt a flash of panic. She wasn't actually sure that she wanted him to kiss her.

His head was bending towards hers when the front door was jerked open and Jack stood there, broad-shouldered and imposing.

'You're home. Great.'

Bryony looked at David. 'Would you like to come in for coffee?'

'He needs to get going,' Jack said coldly, his face unsmiling. 'The roads are icy tonight and they're forecasting snow.'

David was silent for a moment, his eyes on Jack. 'Right. In that case I'd better make a move.'

'OK, then.' Secretly relieved by the decision, Bryony stood on tiptoe and kissed his cheek. 'Thanks for tonight. I enjoyed it.'

'Me, too.' David was still looking at Jack and then he gave a funny smile and turned to Bryony. 'I'll see you at work.'

With that he turned the collar of his coat up and strolled back down her path towards his car.

Bryony followed Jack into the cottage and slipped her coat off.

'I'm sorry Lizzie was such hard work tonight, Jack.' She strolled into the kitchen and flipped the kettle on. 'She never normally wants to call me. And she doesn't normally care if she's lost the book she was reading—she'll just pick another one. It doesn't sound as though you managed to relax at all.'

'I managed.' Jack sank onto one of the kitchen chairs and put his feet on the table in his usual pose. 'I expect she was just a bit unsettled by the thought of you going out with a strange man.'

Bryony frowned slightly. It was Lizzie who had suggested this whole daddy business, so why would she be unsettled? On the other hand, perhaps she hadn't really thought the whole thing through. It was certainly true that Lizzie wasn't used to seeing strange men in her life. She saw Jack and her two uncles and that was about it.

'She'll get used to it.'

'Maybe.' Jack sounded noncommittal. 'So—did you have a good evening?'

There was something in his tone that she couldn't interpret and Bryony lifted two mugs out of the cupboard, not sure how to answer. Had she had a good evening? If she was honest, she didn't really feel she'd had a chance to talk to David. Every time they'd begun a conversation the phone had rung.

Poor Lizzie.

She'd talk to her tomorrow and see how she felt about the whole thing. She certainly didn't want to go on dates if it was going to upset her daughter.

'I had a nice evening,' she said finally, not wanting

to admit to Jack that it had been anything less than perfect. 'It's a shame David wouldn't come in for coffee.'

'It's not a shame. It was a lucky escape.' Jack swung his legs off the table and glared at her. '*Never* invite a man in for coffee.'

Bryony looked at him in astonishment. 'I was being polite.'

He lifted an eyebrow. 'Offering to have sex with a man is being polite?'

Bryony gaped at him, stunned. 'I did not offer to have sex with him, I offered him *coffee.*'

'It's the same thing.' A muscle flickered in his jaw, rough with stubble so late in the evening. He looked dark and dangerous and Bryony felt her stomach flip.

Why couldn't she find David even *half* as attractive? She'd been less than enthusiastic at the possibility of him kissing her, but if it had been Jack who'd been on the doorstep with her...

Reminding herself that she wasn't supposed to be noticing Jack, Bryony picked up the coffee-jar.

'Coffee is the same as sex?' She twisted the jar in her hand, looking at it with a mocking expression. 'Full of caffeine and sold in supermarkets. I don't think so.'

Jack glared at her. 'You can joke about it, but do you really think a man wants to sit around, drinking your coffee?'

'You're sitting around, drinking my coffee,' Bryony pointed out logically, and his mouth hardened.

'That's different. I'm not trying to get you into my bed.'

More's the pity, Bryony thought wistfully, putting the coffee down on the side. If Jack ever tried to get her into his bed she'd be there like a flash.

'Jack, I'm sure David didn't have anything immoral on his mind.'

'Which just shows how little you know about men,' Jack said tightly. 'Do you know the average man thinks about sex every six seconds?'

'So presumably that's why they say men are like photocopiers,' Bryony said dryly. 'Good for reproduction but not much else.'

For once Jack didn't laugh and she sighed inwardly. There was obviously something about the idea of her dating that short-circuited his sense of humour.

Suddenly she wanted the old Jack back. The Jack that called her Blondie and teased her unmercifully. The Jack with the wicked smile and the sexiest wink known to woman.

'Jack.' Her tone was patient. 'I invited David in for coffee because I was being polite. I had no intention of having sex with him.'

'And what if he'd decided to have sex with you?'

She looked at him in exasperation. 'Well, despite the colour of my hair I do have a brain and a mouth,' she said tartly. 'I can think no and say no. At the same time. Amazing really. If I concentrate really hard I can add two and two. Jack, *what is the matter with you?*'

'I just think you're being naïve.'

'Inviting a guy in for coffee?' Bryony gritted her teeth and shook her head. 'You've gone crazy, do you know that?'

There was a long silence and streaks of colour touched his hard cheekbones. 'Maybe I have,' he said shortly, putting his half-full mug on the table and rising to his feet in a fluid movement. 'I'd better get home.'

'Fine. Thank you for babysitting.'

'You're welcome.'

As a farewell it had none of its usual warmth and Bryony turned away and poured the rest of her coffee down the sink, boiling with frustration and feeling confused and upset.

She heard Jack stride to her front door, heard him pick up his jacket and car keys and then the front door slammed behind him.

Bryony winced and let out a long breath.

Just what was going on with Jack?

Bryony was nervous about working with Jack the next day but he seemed back to his usual self, relaxed and good-humoured as they sat in the staffroom and discussed the shifts for Bonfire Night.

'It's my turn.' Sean Nicholson, one of the other consultants, looked at Jack with a resigned expression on his face. 'You deserve a year off from Bonfire Night. You've had a bad few years.'

Jack rolled his eyes. 'I won't know what to do with myself,' he drawled, and Bryony gave him a sympathetic smile.

'You hate this time of year, don't you?'

'I've just seen too many kids with burns after handling fireworks,' he said grimly, scribbling something on his pad. 'OK, so Blondie and I are officially off that night, but if you need us you can call us.' He looked at Bryony. 'Would you be able to come in that night if we needed you?'

Bryony nodded. 'After eight. I'm taking Lizzie to her bonfire party.'

Jack stared at her, his body suddenly unnaturally still. 'What bonfire party?'

'Her friend is having a few sparklers in the garden. Nothing dramatic,' Bryony assured him, but he shook his head.

'No way.' His jaw was tense. 'She shouldn't be going.'

Bryony sighed. 'She's seven, Jack. She wants to be with her friends.'

'So? Invite them all out for a hamburger.'

'It's just a few fireworks and drinks for the parents. It will be over by eight.'

He let out a breath. 'All right. But I'm coming with you.'

'Jack—'

'I'm off and I'm bored.' His blue eyes glittered dangerously. 'It's that or she doesn't go.'

'You're not her father, Jack!' Suddenly remembering that Sean was still in the room, Bryony coloured with embarrassment and shot them an apologetic look. 'Sorry, you guys.'

'No problem,' Sean said easily, 'and I'm sure we won't need you here so just go and have a good time.'

'Great. That's what we'll do, then.'

Jack ran through the rest of the rota and Sean left the room.

Bryony looked at him. 'So what are you planning to do? Bring the fire brigade?'

'When you've spent as long working in A and E

as I have, you won't let your daughter go to domestic firework parties,' he said tightly. 'It's fine. I'll come, too. And you can tell Lizzie's friend's mother that I want a bucket of sand and another bucket of water handy.'

'Why don't we just have an ambulance on standby, just in case?' Bryony suggested tartly. 'Anne's mother will think I've gone barmy.'

'Better barmy than burned.' Jack strode to the door. 'What time does it start?'

'We're getting there at five-thirty for tea and then fireworks,' Bryony said wearily, and Jack nodded.

'Right. I'll pick you both up at five-fifteen. And I want Lizzie in gloves. She's not touching a sparkler with her bare hands.'

Bryony stood up and followed him out of the staff-room, wanting to argue but knowing that he was only being cautious.

He had dealt with a huge number of burns on Bonfire Night, all of which could have been avoided.

And he did adore Lizzie.

Deciding that she should be grateful that he was so protective of her daughter, she picked up a set of notes and called the next patient from the waiting room.

And secretly part of her was excited at spending an evening with Jack. Even if it was in the company of half a dozen parents and their offspring.

It would be lovely to have him there, even though nothing was going to happen.

Reminding herself that Jack was not the man she was dating, she sat down in her chair and waited for the patient to arrive.

CHAPTER FOUR

THE NIGHT of the bonfire party was freezing cold and Bryony pulled on her jeans and thickest jumper and wore her long black coat.

Lizzie was wearing a bright pink hat, pink tights and a pink fleece, and Jack blinked when he arrived to pick them up.

'How are my girls?' He picked Lizzie up and planted a kiss on her cheek. 'You're looking very pink, angel.' He spoke in that lazy drawl that sent butterflies flitting through Bryony's stomach. 'Do you have any pink gloves to go with that outfit, sweetheart?'

'Somewhere.'

Jack smiled and put her back down. 'Find them for me, there's a good girl.' He looked at Bryony and she smiled, determined to have a nice evening.

'Is my dress decent enough for you, Jack?'

For a moment he didn't react and then he laughed. 'Exactly the way I like it. None of you showing.'

Bryony rolled her eyes and tried not to be offended that he didn't actually want to see any of her body. Obviously she was lacking in something, or he would have pounced on her long ago.

Lizzie came back into the hall, holding her gloves, and Jack nodded.

'Good girl.' He opened the front door and led them towards his car. 'Now, Lizzie, tonight when the fireworks start, I want you to stay by me. The whole time. OK?'

'But what if I want to play with my friends?'

'You can play with them before and after,' he said firmly, strapping her into her seat. 'But during the fireworks, you stay with me.'

Lizzie's eyes were huge and solemn. 'Are you very afraid of them, Jack? Will I need to hold your hand?'

Bryony smothered a giggle but Jack's expression didn't flicker. 'I'm terrified of them, angel. And I'm relying on you to be beside me.'

'I'll be there the whole time,' Lizzie assured him, and Bryony rolled her eyes as she slid into the passenger seat, knowing that Jack had got his own way.

Lizzie's friend Anne lived in a house with a huge garden and they arrived to find that the trees had been decorated with fairy lights and everyone was gathered round, laughing and waiting for sausages to cook.

It felt wintry and cold, and delicious smells wafted through the freezing air.

'Hello, Lizzie.' Anne's mother greeted them warmly and drew them into the garden, introducing them to people they didn't know.

'Where have you stored the fireworks?' was Jack's first question, and Bryony put a hand on his arm and smiled at Anne's mother.

'Jack is a consultant in A and E,' she explained hastily, 'and we doctors are always a bit nervous of fireworks. Take no notice.'

'Anne's father has it all under control,' the woman assured them, waving a hand towards the bottom of the garden. 'The children won't be allowed near them. Apart from the sparklers, of course.'

Bryony saw Jack's mouth open and quickly spoke before he did. 'That's great,' she said cheerfully, her fingers biting into his arm like a vice. 'Those sausages smell fantastic.'

'Well, we're just about ready to eat.' Anne's mother led them to a table loaded with food. 'Grab yourself a roll and some ketchup and tuck in!'

She walked away and Jack scowled at Bryony. 'You just made holes in my arm.'

'I was trying to stop you embarrassing Lizzie,' she hissed, smiling sweetly at one of the mothers who passed. 'Now, eat something and relax. Try and remember that you only see the disasters in A and E. You don't see the normal, happy bonfire parties that everyone enjoys.'

There was a long silence and then, to her surprise, Jack sucked in a breath and gave her a lopsided smile. 'You're right,' he said dryly, running a hand through his cropped dark hair. 'I'm being an idiot. It's just that I love Lizzie so much.'

Bryony's face softened. 'I know you do.' On impulse she stood on tiptoe and kissed his cheek, feeling the roughness of stubble against her lips and smelling the sexy male smell that was Jack.

He looked startled. 'What was that for?'

'For being you.' Deciding that, for a girl who was supposed to be forgetting about Jack, she wasn't actually doing that well, Bryony left him by the bread rolls and went and found Lizzie.

'You kissed Jack.' Lizzie was looking at her curiously and Bryony felt herself blush.

'Just on the cheek,' she said hastily, and Lizzie tipped her head on one side.

'Jack would make a cool dad.'

Pretending that she hadn't heard that remark, Bryony turned to chat to one of the mothers that she knew vaguely, trying not to look at Jack who was now deep in conversation with one of the prettiest mothers in the school. He looked broad-shouldered and powerful with his back to her, and her stomach twisted as she saw the woman laughing up at him flirtatiously.

Reminding herself that she was supposed to be getting a life and forgetting about Jack, Bryony joined in with the others, handing food to the children, topping up drinks and wiping ketchup from faces.

Anne's father lit the bonfire and the flames licked towards the dark sky, suddenly illuminating the massive garden.

'You kids stay here,' he ordered cheerfully. 'I'm going to start the show.'

'Mummy, can I have another drink?' Lizzie tugged at her sleeve, her cheeks pink from the cold, and Bryony took her hand and led her over to the table.

'What do you want?' She picked up some empty cartons and then found a full one. 'Apple juice OK?'

'Great.' Lizzie took the cup and looked around her happily. 'Isn't this great, Mummy? You, me and Jack together.'

Bryony swallowed. 'Well, er, we're not exactly…' Then she smiled weakly. 'Yes, sweetheart, it's great.'

There were shrieks of excitement from the other children as they played closer to the fire and Bryony felt a stab of unease.

They were too close…

Opening her mouth to caution them, she noticed

the other parents laughing, totally relaxed, and closed her mouth again. She really must try and act like a normal parent and not like a doctor, seeing accidents everywhere.

'Can I go and play, Mummy?' Lizzie put her drink down and moved towards the other children, but Bryony grabbed her arm, struck by a premonition so powerful that it made her gasp. 'No, Lizzie. I think—'

Before she could even finish her sentence there was a series of horrific screams from Annie, and Bryony saw flames engulfing her little body with frightening speed.

'Oh, my God—*Jack*!' Bryony screamed his name at the top of her voice and ran forward, dragging off her coat as she ran.

Jack was there before her, knocking the girl to the ground and covering her with his jacket. 'Cold water—get me cold water *now*!' His voice was harsh and everyone ran to do as he said while Bryony stood there, so shocked she could hardly move.

All Jack's attention was on the injured girl. 'It's going to be all right, sweetheart. You're going to be fine.' Jack lifted his head and looked straight at one of the fathers. 'Call the paramedics and get me a hosepipe and cling film. Blondie, I need your help with her clothes.'

Bryony still didn't move.

'Dr Hunter.' His voice was sharp. 'I need your help here.'

His sharp reminder of her profession brought her back to reality. She nodded and breathed deeply, try- ing to forget that it was Annie lying on the ground.

Her daughter's friend.

Annie's mother was screaming hysterically and clinging to the other mothers while two of the fathers had fortunately listened to Jack's orders and rolled out a hosepipe.

'OK, sweetheart, you're going to be fine.' Jack carried on talking to Annie, his voice gentle and reassuring as he removed his jacket from the injured girl and took the end of the hosepipe.

Bryony dropped on her knees beside him. 'What do you want me to do?'

She felt physically sick but as usual Jack was rock-solid and totally calm.

'Her clothes are smouldering. If they're not actually stuck to her body, I want them off.'

He turned the hose onto Annie's body, the cold water taking the heat away from the burn as Bryony struggled to remove the clothing.

'Get me scissors.'

Someone quickly produced a pair and she cut the clothing away as gently as she could, careful not to disturb any that actually adhered to the burn.

'It's all below her waist,' Jack said softly, his eyes assessing the area of the burn. 'It's the skirt area. Her skirt caught fire. Has someone called the ambulance?'

'I did, Jack,' Lizzie said in a shaky voice from right beside them. 'They said they'd be here in two minutes.'

'Good girl.' Jack gave her a nod of approval. 'Sweetheart, I need some clingfilm. The stuff you wrap round food in the kitchen. The women over there are too upset to help and the men seem to have forgotten. Can you find it for me, angel?'

Lizzie nodded and shot down the garden towards the house, legs and arms pumping. She was back in less than a minute with a long, thin box.

'That's my girl. Now open it up for me,' Jack ordered, and Lizzie fished it out awkwardly and struggled to find the end.

'How much do you want?'

'I'll do it, Lizzie.' Bryony took it from her, worried about her daughter seeing her friend so badly injured. 'You can go into the house with the other children.'

'I want to help.'

They heard the sound of an ambulance approaching and Jack looked at Lizzie. 'Go and meet them. Tell them I want oxygen, two large-bore cannulae, IV fluids and morphine. Have you got that?'

Lizzie nodded and Bryony glanced at him.

'She won't remember that, Jack, she's only seven.'

'She'll remember,' Jack said firmly, his eyes fixed on Lizzie. 'Oxygen, two large-bore cannulae, IV fluids and morphine. Go, angel.'

Lizzie sped back down the garden to meet the ambulance, leaving Jack and Bryony to wrap the exposed burns.

'Can you get us clean sheets?' Bryony addressed one of the fathers who was hovering by helplessly.

'And someone put that bonfire out,' Jack added, checking Annie's pulse and breathing.

She'd stopped screaming and was lying shivering, sobbing quietly, her father by her side.

Annie's mother was still hysterical at the far side of the garden.

Seconds later the paramedics arrived with Lizzie,

complete with all the equipment that Jack had asked for.

As Bryony grabbed the oxygen and fitted the mask gently to Annie's face, Jack smiled at Lizzie, his blue eyes showering her with approval and warmth.

'Good girl.'

Despite the stress of the situation Lizzie returned the smile bravely and Jack gave a nod.

'All right, I'm going to need your help here, Lizzie. Annie needs some fluid and we're going to put a line in and give her fluid through her arm. Then we're going to take her to hospital. I want you to hold this for me.'

Bryony looked at him uncertainly, still not sure that her young daughter should be exposed to the harsh realities of immediate care, but Jack seemed determined to involve her and Lizzie was frowning with concentration as she listened carefully to Jack's instructions and did as he asked.

Too worried about little Annie to argue, Bryony turned her attention back to the little girl, following Jack's instructions to the letter.

'Shall I give her morphine?'

'We're going to give it IV.' Jack murmured, picking up a cannula and searching for a vein. 'Can you squeeze for me?'

Bryony took Annie's little arm and squeezed, praying that Jack would find a vein first time.

He did, of course, and she breathed a sigh of relief.

'Give her the morphine and cyclizine in there and then we'll put a line in the other arm, too,' Jack said, holding out a hand for the syringe that the paramedic was holding ready. 'OK, sweetheart.' He looked down at Annie, his eyes gentle. 'This is going to make you feel better, I promise. And then we're going to take you to hospital. You're doing fine. You're brilliant.'

He gave the morphine and then put a cannula into the other arm and looked at Bryony. 'OK, let's get some fluid into her and get her covered or she'll get hypothermia from the cold water.'

He and Bryony worked together, each anticipating the other's needs, until finally the little girl was stabilised and in the ambulance.

'I'll go with her,' Jack said. 'Meet me at the hospital when you've dropped Lizzie at your mother's.'

'I want to come, too,' Lizzie said firmly, and Bryony shook her head.

'Sweetheart, no.'

'Bring her,' Jack said firmly. 'I'll run her home later. She can wait in the staffroom.'

He dug in his pocket and produced his car keys, a wry smile playing around his firm mouth. 'If you prang my car, Blondie, you're history.' Handing the keys to Lizzie, he jerked his head towards the front of the house. 'Go and wait for your mother by the car, sweetheart.'

Lizzie did as she was told and Jack took Bryony by the shoulders, forcing her to look at him. 'She's just seen her best friend horribly burned,' he said quietly. 'That is going to stay with her a long time and will be easier to bear if she knows she did something to help. Trust me on this one. She's tough, our Lizzie. She'll be fine. But do it my way.'

Bryony swallowed and nodded, knowing that whatever they did now the trauma had already happened for Lizzie. Maybe it was best for her to be involved.

Anne's parents came over, her mother clinging to her husband, her face streaked with tears.

'Can we go in the ambulance with her?'

Jack exchanged glances with one of the paramedics and then nodded. 'Of course. But try and be calm. I know it's a terrible shock but she needs you to be strong. If she sees you panicking, then she'll panic, and I don't want her any more scared than she is already.'

Bryony waited while they loaded Annie into the ambulance and then she joined Lizzie by Jack's car.

She pressed the remote to unlock the door and gave a short laugh. Now she knew it was an emergency. There was no other reason that Jack would have let her near his precious sports car—he never let anyone drive it.

She strapped Lizzie in the front seat and slid into the driver's seat, telling herself that it was only a car. Exactly like her car really, except that it was capable of ridiculous speed and cost about fifteen times as much.

She started the engine and flinched as the car gave a throaty growl. 'Boys with toys,' she muttered disparagingly, finding first gear and carefully pulling out of the driveway onto the road. She just hoped she didn't meet any other traffic on the way to hospital.

When she arrived she settled Lizzie in the staff-room, promising to come back and update her as soon as possible.

Jack was already in Resus, along with Sean

Nicholson and a full team of staff. Jack was barking out instructions as he worked to stabilise Annie.

'Can someone check her weight with her parents?'

'I've just done it.' Bryony hurried into the room and reached in her pocket for a calculator. 'I've worked out 4 mils of fluid per kilogram multiplied by the percentage of the burn. Do you have that yet?'

'Just doing it. My estimate is twenty-two per cent,' Jack said, glancing up at her. 'Are you OK?'

Bryony nodded and studied the Lund and Browder charts that helped them to assess the area of the burn according to age. 'You're about right, Jack,' she said lightly, feeding the numbers into her calculator. 'I make it twenty-two per cent.'

She worked out the volume of fluid and showed her calculation to Jack.

'Right.' He gave a nod. 'So she needs that in twenty-four hours, but we need to give her half in the first eight hours and monitor her urine output. I want her to have a combination of crystalloid and colloid.'

'Catheter is in,' Nicky said quickly, 'and I've started a chart.'

'Great. Can you test her urine? And, Bryony, we need to take some bloods before she's transferred. Cross-matching, FBC, COHb, U and Es, glucose and coagulation.'

Bryony reached for the appropriate bottles. 'You're sending her to the burns unit?'

Jack nodded. 'The helicopter is waiting to take her as soon as we give the word. I've spoken to the consultant, he's waiting for her.'

Bryony took the samples and then went to talk to

Annie. The little girl was drifting in and out of sleep, hardly aware of what was going on around her.

'I gave her some sedation,' Jack said softly, covering the last of the burns and then giving Nicky a nod. 'OK. Let's go.'

'Are you going with her?'

He nodded. 'Take Lizzie home in my car. I'll see you later.'

'How will you get home?'

'I'll get the paramedics to drop me at your place, or I'll grab a taxi.' He shrugged, totally unconcerned, and she nodded.

'Fine. I'll see you later. Do you want me to talk to Annie's parents?'

'I'll do it,' Sean said immediately. 'That way you can get home with your little girl and Jack can get loaded into the helicopter.'

Bryony was tucking Lizzie into bed when she heard the doorbell. 'That will be Jack.'

She dropped a kiss on Lizzie's forehead and went to answer the door, praying that Annie's condition hadn't worsened during the transfer.

'How is she?'

Jack strolled into her house and gave a shiver, and it was only then that she remembered that he'd used his jacket to put out the flames and that he'd been working only in a jumper. He must be freezing.

'Come and sit by the fire,' she urged, and he did as she'd suggested, stretching out his hands towards the flames.

'It's nice and warm in here.' He looked at her. 'Is my girl asleep?'

Bryony shook her head, her expression troubled. 'No. She's very upset by it all.'

'Of course she is.' His jaw tightened. 'I'll talk to her.'

They both walked towards Lizzie's bedroom and Jack strolled in and settled himself on the edge of the bed.

'Hi, there.' His voice was soft and Lizzie stared up at him, her eyes huge in her pretty face.

'Hi, Jack.' Her smile was shaky. 'Annie is very badly hurt, isn't she?'

Jack hesitated. 'She is pretty badly hurt,' he agreed, and Bryony mentally thanked him for not lying. She knew that Annie's condition was serious and if anything happened to the little girl, she didn't want Lizzie to feel that they'd been dishonest.

'Is she going to die?' Lizzie's voice trembled and Jack shook his head.

'No, sweetheart. I'm sure she isn't going to die. I've just taken her to a special hospital where they know all about burns.'

'Can I go and see her there?'

'Sure,' Jack said immediately. 'We'll go together.'

Tears suddenly welled up in Lizzie's eyes and Jack immediately leaned forward and lifted the little girl onto his lap.

'Don't cry, baby,' he said roughly, stroking her hair with his strong hand and exchanging an agonised look with Bryony. 'You were brilliant. My little star. All those grown-ups were panicking and you were cool as ice cream.'

Lizzie gave a sniff and pulled away from him, but her little hands still clutched at his jumper. 'I told the paramedics everything you wanted, just like you said.'

'I know you did.' Jack smiled down at her, pride in his eyes. 'You were unbelievable. And I was so proud of you. You really helped save Annie.'

'I helped?' Lizzie's face brightened slightly. 'Really?'

'Really.' Jack nodded, his handsome face serious. 'You see, you did all the right things. Everyone was scared and I bet you were, too, but you didn't let being scared stop you from doing what needed to be done. And that makes you a very special person.'

'It does?'

'Certainly. I don't know many grown-ups who would have been as calm as you and remembered all those things and done what you did.' Jack lifted a hand and stroked Lizzie's blonde curls away from her face. 'One day, if you wanted to, I think you could be a very important doctor.'

Bryony swallowed down a lump in her throat and Lizzie's eyes widened. 'Like you and Mummy?'

Jack grinned. 'Maybe not quite as important as me,' he said teasingly, winking at Bryony who smiled back weakly. 'But important, just the same.'

Lizzie gave a gurgle of laughter and punched him on the shoulder. 'That's boasting, Jack,' she said reprovingly, and wound her arms round his neck. 'I'm glad you and Mummy were there.'

For a brief moment Jack squeezed his eyes shut, his jaw tense, and Bryony knew exactly what was going through his mind. He'd been imagining a scene where he hadn't been there, a scene where there hadn't been a doctor on site to administer first aid, a scene where Lizzie might have been the one near the bonfire.

She gave a little shudder, imagining the same scene, and Jack's eyes opened and locked on hers for a meaningful second.

'Time for you to go to bed now, angel,' he said softly, lifting Lizzie off his lap and tucking her under the covers with her mermaid. He leaned across and switched her little pink lamp on. 'Your mum and I will just be eating some supper in the kitchen. Shout if you want anything.'

'I don't want you to go home tonight.'

'I'm not going,' Jack said immediately, sounding rock-solid, dependable and altogether too male for Bryony's piece of mind. 'Tonight I'm sleeping in your spare room.'

Lizzie gave a smile and they were just tiptoeing to the door when she spoke again.

'Jack?' Lizzie's voice was a little-girl whisper and Bryony saw Jack's face soften.

'Yes, angel.'

'Tomorrow when we wake up, will you play with me?'

Jack grinned. 'Absolutely.'

'Can we play Weddings?'

'My favourite game,' Jack said softly, walking back across the room and bending down to kiss her one more time. 'Now, get some sleep. I can't marry you with black rings under your eyes.'

Lizzie chuckled, sounding much happier. 'Mummy, will you leave the door open?'

'Of course, sweetheart. And I'll pop my head in later.'

Jack followed Bryony out of the room.

'Thank you for that,' she said quietly, walking through to the kitchen and opening the fridge. 'You said all the right things. In fact, you did all the right things, too. My instincts were to just get her out of there.'

'That would have been my instinct, too, if she hadn't already seen her friend engulfed by flames,' Jack said wearily, sinking down on one of her kitchen chairs with a groan. 'To be honest, I was mostly concentrating on Annie, but I did think that if Lizzie knew she'd helped, she might feel better.'

'Which she did.' Bryony removed a bottle of wine from the fridge and handed it to him along with a corkscrew. 'I just hope she doesn't have nightmares.'

'She's a tough kid,' Jack said, yanking the cork out and setting the bottle down on the table. 'She'll be fine. As soon as Annie is a bit better we can take Lizzie along to see her.'

We.

Listening to him talking as if they were a family, Bryony found it harder and harder to remember that she was supposed to not be thinking of Jack in *that* way any more.

Remembering how skilled he'd been with Annie brought a lump to her throat. 'You're amazing, do you know that?' She reached into the cupboard for two glasses, trying to keep her tone light. 'You never lose your cool, no matter what. I just saw Annie on fire and I froze.'

'Only for about three seconds,' Jack said easily, stretching out a hand for the glasses and filling them both to the top. 'And working in a well-equipped

A and E department is very different from immediate care, as you know. Here. Have a drink. I think we both need it.'

'I should cook some supper first.'

'Forget cooking.' Jack took a mouthful of wine and gave a groan of pleasure. 'That's good. Let's send out for pizza or something.'

Bryony giggled. 'I can't do that. Lizzie will find the boxes in the morning and she'll kill me. Pizza is her treat.'

Jack shrugged. 'All right. Indian, then. I left a menu by your phone last time I was here.'

'It would be nice not to cook,' Bryony agreed, and Jack stood up.

'That's decided, then. Indian it is. What do you want?'

Bryony shrugged. 'You choose.'

So he did and the food arrived half an hour later and was wonderful.

They were well into the bottle of wine when they heard Lizzie's screams.

Both of them sprinted to her bedroom to find her sobbing and clutching her mermaid, her face blotched with tears.

'I keep thinking of Annie.'

Bryony cuddled her close, rocking her gently. 'Well, of course you do, darling. Annie is your friend. She's going to be fine, Lizzie.'

As she said the words she prayed that she was right. If anything happened to Annie…

Eventually Lizzie calmed down and fell asleep again and the two of them tiptoed back to the kitchen.

Bryony felt totally stressed and she was seriously

worried about the effect of the accident on her daughter. As Jack had rightly said, she'd actually seen it happen. What sort of impact would that have on her in the long term?

She desperately wanted to lean on Jack but she couldn't bring herself to ask him for the hug she so badly needed.

And then he looked at her and she knew he felt the same way. 'I hate Bonfire Night.'

His voice was hoarse and for the first time Bryony caught a glimpse of the strain he must have been under.

She gave a little frown. 'We forget about you, Jack,' she said softly, stepping up to him and looking at him with concern in her eyes. 'You always seem so strong—so much the one in charge. Everyone else is panicking and flapping and you're so calm. It's easy to forget that you can be affected by things, too.'

'Hey.' He gave a sexy grin that belied the strain in his eyes. 'I'm Mr Tough.'

She smiled. 'Well, would Mr Tough like a cup of coffee?'

'As I'm not driving, I'd rather finish the wine,' he admitted ruefully, reaching for his glass. 'Do you mind me staying?'

'Of course not,' she said blithely, wondering why her heart was thumping so hard. Jack had stayed in her cottage on numerous occasions. Why did this time feel different?

'I'll get you some stuff ready,' she said formally, and he reached out and grabbed her arm.

'Don't bother. I don't wear anything in bed anyway.'

Bryony swallowed hard, trying to dispel the mental image of Jack naked in her spare room.

For a woman who was not supposed to be thinking about Jack Rothwell, she was failing dismally.

'Jack…'

'What I really need is a hug.' Without waiting for a response, he hauled her against him and she went into his arms, feeling the softness of his jumper covering the hard muscle of his chest and the strength of his arms as he held her. He gave a groan and tightened his hold, burying his face in her hair.

Bryony could hardly breathe. She felt the steady thud of his heart against her flushed cheek, felt her whole body tingle in response to the feel of his body against hers. He felt strong and safe and deliciously male.

They stood like that for a moment and she closed her eyes, wishing that it could last for ever. Wishing that it could lead to something more.

And then gradually his grip on her loosened and his hands slid slowly up her arms. His strong fingers curled into her shoulders and he looked down at her, his blue eyes suddenly intent on her face.

A warmth spread slowly through her pelvis and her whole body melted with longing.

She felt his fingers tighten, saw something flicker in her eyes and then his head lowered towards hers.

He was going to kiss her.

Finally, after so many years of dreaming about exactly that, Jack was going to kiss her.

Dizzy with excitement, Bryony stared up at him, breathless with anticipation.

And then suddenly his hands fell away from her

shoulders and he stepped back, his handsome face blank of expression.

'We should probably get some sleep, Blondie.' His tone was light and he glanced at the clock on the wall. 'It's getting late.'

Bryony tried to smile but it was a poor effort. She felt swamped with a disappointment so powerful that it was almost a physical pain. *She'd been so sure that he was going to kiss her.*

But why would Jack kiss her?

She gritted her teeth, furious with herself. She was doing it again. Fantasising about Jack.

So much for her campaign to date other men. So far she'd been on one date that had been an utter disaster and she was still noticing Jack.

She had less than two months to find Lizzie a daddy, or at least someone who looked as though he had potential. It was time she made more effort.

She needed to kiss someone and see if that helped.

She needed to stop comparing everyone with Jack.

There must be another man who looked good in jeans. There must be another man who always knew exactly what to do when everyone around them was panicking. There must be another man who would make her knees wobble every time he walked into a room.

And she was going to find him.

CHAPTER FIVE

THE rest of November flew past and Annie's condition gradually improved.

'The burns are almost all round her skirt area,' Jack told Bryony one day as they snatched a quick cup of coffee during a late shift. 'I talked to the consultant last night. She's going to need extensive skin grafts.'

'Poor mite.' Bryony pulled a face at the thought of the number of hospital stays Annie was going to have to endure. 'It's going to be so hard for her.'

Jack nodded. 'But at least she's alive. And Lizzie seems to have bounced back amazingly well.'

'Yes.' Bryony smiled. 'I was worried about that but she's doing fine. We're visiting Annie a lot, which helps, and Lizzie has made it her mission to act as the link between Annie and the school. She's been taking her all sorts of books and things to do and generally keeping her in touch with the gossip.'

'She's a great girl.' Jack drained his coffee and sat back in his chair with a yawn, long legs stretched out in front of him. 'So, Blondie. December the first tomorrow.'

Bryony stared gloomily into her coffee. 'Don't remind me. I now have less than a month to sort out Lizzie's Christmas present, and I'm fast coming to the conclusion that it's an impossible task.'

Jack looked at her quizzically, a strange light in his

eyes. 'So, is the romance with David Armstrong not working?'

Romance?

Bryony looked at him. 'We've been on two dates. The first one we barely had time to talk because you kept calling—not that it was your fault that Lizzie was demanding that night,' she added hastily, hoping that he didn't think that she was complaining, 'and the second date was disturbed because you called him back to the hospital to see a child. And that wasn't your fault either.'

Jack looked at her, his expression inscrutable. 'And he hasn't asked you out since?'

'Well, funnily enough, he rang me this morning,' Bryony confided, 'and he's taking me to dinner at The Peacock on Saturday. Neither of us is on call and Lizzie is sleeping at my mother's so this time there should be absolutely no interruptions.'

And this time she was going to kiss him.

She'd made up her mind that she was going to kiss him.

She was utterly convinced that kissing another man would cure her obsession with Jack.

David was a good-looking guy. She knew that lots of the nurses lusted after him secretly. He must know how to kiss.

And it was going to happen on Saturday. She was going to invite him in for coffee and she was going to kiss him.

The next day was incredibly busy.

'It's the roads,' Sean said wearily as they snatched a five-minute coffee-break in the middle of a long and intensive shift. 'They're so icy and people drive too fast. I predict a nasty pile-up before the end of the evening.'

His prediction proved correct.

At seven o'clock the ambulance hotline rang. Bryony answered it and when she finally put the phone down both Sean and Jack were watching her expectantly.

'Are you clairvoyant?' She looked at Sean who shrugged.

'Black ice. It was inevitable. What are the details?'

'Twenty-two-year-old female, conscious but shocked and complaining of chest pains.'

She'd barely finished repeating what Ambulance Control had told her when the doors slammed open and the paramedics hurried in with the trolley.

'Straight into Resus,' Jack ordered and they transferred the woman onto the trolley as smoothly as possible. While the rest of the team moved quickly into action he questioned the paramedics about the accident.

'It was a side impact,' the paramedic told him. 'She was driving and the other vehicle went straight into her side. Her passenger walked away virtually unharmed. He's giving her details to Reception now.'

Jack nodded and turned his attention back to the young woman, a frown on his face. 'She has a neck haematoma. I want a chest X-ray, fast,' he murmured, and looked at Bryony. 'Have you got a line in?'

She nodded. 'One.'

'Put in another one,' he ordered, 'but hold the fluid. And cross-match ten units of blood.'

Bryony's eyes widened. 'Why?'

'Just a feeling. Nicky, I want a BP from both arms,' he said, gesturing to the staff to stand back while the radiographer took the chest film.

'Her blood pressure is different in each arm,' Nicky said quickly, and Jack nodded.

'I thought it might be. She's only slightly hypotensive so I want minimal fluid replacement for now.'

Bryony looked at him, waiting for a blonde joke or one of his usual quips that would ease the tension, but this time his eyes were fixed on the patient.

'Fast-bleep the surgeons,' he ordered, 'and let's take a look at that chest X-ray.'

They walked across to look at the chest X-ray and Bryony looked at him, able to talk now that they were away from the patient. 'Why did you cross-match so much blood?'

'Because I think she's ruptured her aorta.'

Bryony's eyes widened. 'But a ruptured aorta has a 90 per cent mortality rate. She'd be dead.'

He squinted at the X-ray. 'Unless the bleed is contained by the aortic adventitia. Then she'd be alive. But at risk of haemorrhage.'

Bryony stared at the X-ray, too, and Jack lifted an eyebrow.

'OK, Blondie—impress me. What do you see?'

'The mediastinum is widened.'

'And is that significant?'

Bryony chewed her lip and delved into her brain. 'On its own, possibly not,' she said, remembering something she'd read, 'but taken with other factors…'

'Such as?'

Bryony looked again, determined not to miss anything. 'The trachea is deviated to the right. The aortic outline is blurred and the aortic knuckle is obliterated.'

'What else?'

'It's cloudy.' She peered closer at the X-ray. 'I haven't seen that before. Is it a haemothorax?'

'Full marks.' He gave her a lazy smile but his eyes glittered with admiration. 'She has a right-sided haemothorax caused by a traumatic rupture of the thoracic aorta, which is currently contained. In this case we can see it clearly on the X-ray, but not always.'

Bryony looked at him and felt her heart thud harder. The patient was lucky to be alive. 'So what happens now?'

'She needs urgent surgical repair. In the meantime, we need to give fluid cautiously, otherwise the adventitia could rupture and she'll have a fatal haemorrhage.'

'So presumably we also need to give her good pain relief so that her blood pressure doesn't go up?'

His eyes rested on her shiny blonde hair and he shook his head solemnly. 'Amazing.'

She poked her tongue out discreetly and he gave her a sexy smile that made her knees wobble.

Fortunately, at that moment the surgeons walked into the room and provided a distraction. They all conferred, agreeing to take the woman to Theatre right away for surgical repair.

'So what exactly do they do?' Bryony asked Jack after the woman had been safely handed over to the surgeons and they were left to deal with the debris in Resus.

'Depends.' He ripped off his gloves and dropped them into the bin. 'They'll attempt a surgical repair.'

'And if they can't repair it?'

'Then they'll do a vascular graft.'

Bryony helped Nicky to clean the trolley. 'But what made you suspect an aortic rupture? I always thought patients died at the scene of the accident.'

'Well, if they're alive it basically suggests a partial injury,' he told her. 'It's often hard to diagnose on X-ray. A widened mediastinum doesn't necessarily indicate an abnormality. But in her case there were other classic chest X-ray signs and she had clinical signs too. The neck haematoma, asymmetric BP and chest pain.'

'And if the X-ray hadn't been clear?'

'I would have talked to the consultant radiologist and we would have done a multi-slice CT scan. It's worth finding out as much as you can about the details of the accident. The paramedic told us her car had been hit on the driver's side. A significant number of blunt traumatic aortic ruptures are caused by side impact.'

Bryony stared at him in fascination. 'What's the pathology?'

'Basically a sudden deceleration such as a fall from a height or an RTA allows the mobile parts of the aorta to keep moving. It usually tears where the aorta is tethered to the pulmonary vein—'

'The ligamentum arteriosum,' Bryony intervened, and he rolled his eyes.

'If there's one thing I can't stand, it's a brainy blonde,' he drawled, and she clucked sympathetically.

'If I'm threatening your ego then just let me know.'

'My ego is shivering,' he assured her, his blue eyes twinkling as looked down at her. 'What do you get when you give a blonde a penny for her thoughts?'

'Change,' Bryony said immediately, tilting her head to one side. 'Why is a man like a vintage wine?'

Jack's eyes narrowed and his mouth twitched. 'Go on…'

'Because they all start out like grapes,' Bryony said cheerfully, 'and it's a woman's job to tread all over them and keep them in the dark until they mature into something you'd like to have dinner with.'

Nicky gave a snort of amusement from the corner of the room and Jack grinned.

'That's shockingly sexist, Blondie.'

'Just giving as good as I get.'

Jack's smile faded. 'And talking about having dinner, haven't you got a date tomorrow night?'

'Yes.' Bryony frowned as she remembered that she had all of three weeks to find a man who might make a good father for Lizzie. By anyone's standards it was a tall order.

But at least she had another date with David so he must be fairly keen.

And he was a really nice man. Her eyes slid to Jack's face and then away again. She wasn't going to compare him to Jack. All right, so Jack was staggeringly handsome and he was clever and he had a great sense of humour— She cut herself off before the list grew too long. Jack didn't do commitment. And Jack didn't notice her. Which ruled him out as a potential partner.

At least David noticed her.

And she was going to start noticing him, she told

herself firmly, leaving the room so that she wouldn't be tempted to continually look at Jack.

'I'm really looking forward to tonight.' Bryony slid into David's car and gave him a smile. 'The food is meant to be great and Lizzie is at my mother's so we are guaranteed no interruptions.'

David waited while she fastened her seat belt and then pulled out of her drive. 'Let's hope not.'

They walked into the restaurant ten minutes later and Bryony gave a gasp of delight as she saw the Christmas tree sparkling by the log fire. 'Oh—it's lovely.'

And romantic.

How could she and David fail to further their relationship in this atmosphere?

It was made for lovers.

She handed over her coat, feeling David's eyes slide over her.

'You look great,' he said quietly, and she smiled shyly, pleased that she'd bought the red dress she'd seen on a shopping expedition a week earlier.

'So do you.'

And he did. He was wearing a dark, well-cut suit and she saw several female heads turn towards him as they were shown to their table.

All right, so he didn't make her knees wobble but that was a good thing surely. With Jack she actually felt physically sick every time he walked into a room, which was utterly ridiculous. She couldn't concentrate and she couldn't breathe. All she was aware of was him. And that wasn't what she wanted in a stable, long-term relationship.

At least being with David didn't make her feel sick with excitement.

They ordered their food and then David picked up his glass and raised it. 'To an uninterrupted evening.'

She smiled and lifted her glass in response but before she could speak she gave a gasp of surprise. 'Oh—it's Jack!'

David's jaw tightened and he put his glass carefully down on the table. *'Jack?'*

'Jack Rothwell. He's just walked in with some blonde.'

Bryony felt a flash of jealousy as she studied Jack's companion. She was his usual type. Endless legs, silvery blonde hair and a skirt that barely covered her bottom. She wore a very low-cut top and Bryony glanced at Jack to see signs of disapproval, but he seemed perfectly relaxed, his eyes twinkling flirtatiously as he laughed at something the girl had said.

By contrast, David was glowering, his earlier good humour seemingly gone as he reached for his wine.

'Well…' Bryony made a determined effort not to look at Jack and not to mind that he didn't appear to have noticed her anyway. 'That's a coincidence.'

'Is it?' David's eyes glittered ominously and he sat back in his chair as the waiter poured more wine into his glass. 'Aren't you beginning to wonder why it is that Jack Rothwell would want to sabotage every date we have?'

'Sabotage?' Bryony looked at him in astonishment and gave a puzzled laugh. 'Jack has nothing to do with the fact that our last two dates haven't worked out that well.'

'No?'

'Well, he's certainly not sabotaging tonight,' Bryony said reasonably. 'I mean, he hasn't even noticed we're here. He's with a woman himself.'

She glanced across the restaurant again and immediately wished she hadn't. Jack was leaning forward, his attention totally focused on his beautiful companion.

Bryony looked away quickly, trying not to mind. Knowing that she had no right to mind.

And, anyway, she was with David.

But he was looking at her with an odd expression on his face. 'He knows you're here,' he said quietly, 'and no man could fail to notice you, Bryony.'

She blushed at the compliment. 'Well, that's very kind of you, but I can assure you that Jack certainly doesn't notice me in the way you're suggesting.'

In fact, he didn't seem to notice her as a woman at all. Until she wore something that he disapproved of, she thought gloomily. Goodness knew how he would have reacted had she been the one dressed like his date. He probably would have had her locked up. But evidently the girl staring into his eyes at that precise moment was allowed to dress however she pleased.

Realising that she was staring again, Bryony turned her attention back to David but the atmosphere had changed. She made a valiant attempt to keep up lively conversation but it seemed like hard work.

In the end they ate their starter in virtual silence and Bryony's gaze flickered surreptitiously to Jack yet again.

Immediately their eyes locked and she swallowed hard, aware that he must have been looking at her.

His eyes held hers and everything and everyone else in the room gradually faded into the background. For Bryony there was just Jack and he seemed as reluctant to break the contact as she was.

Her heart banged against her ribs with rhythmic force and the sick feeling started in her stomach.

And still Jack's eyes held hers.

They might have stared at each other for ever if the waiter hadn't chosen that moment to deliver their next course, walking across their line of vision.

Staring down at her plate, Bryony realised that suddenly she wasn't hungry any more. Her insides felt totally jumbled up.

Why had Jack been staring at her like that?

Did he disapprove of her seeing David? Did he think that she was dating the wrong man?

She pushed her food around her plate, miserably aware that David had finished his main course and was now watching her in silence.

Finally he spoke. 'You don't seem hungry.'

'Not very.' She put her fork down and smiled at him apologetically. 'I'm so sorry.'

'It doesn't matter.'

She bit her lip, embarrassed that the evening was going so badly. 'I'm just a bit tired—it's been a pretty busy week.'

'Do you want to go home?'

She hesitated and then nodded. 'Yes. If that's all right with you.'

'Shall we have coffee first?'

She remembered her resolution to kiss him. 'No,' she croaked. 'Let's have coffee at my house.'

He looked at her thoughtfully and seemed to relax

slightly. Then he nodded and rose to his feet. 'Good idea. Come on. I'll settle the bill while they get our coats.'

'If you've finished, I'll take her home.' Jack's deep voice came from right beside her, his eyes fixed on her face. 'It's on my way.'

The two men stared at each other with ill-disguised hostility.

'She's my date,' David said tightly, and Jack smiled.

'You've had your date,' he drawled softly, 'and now I'm taking her home.'

Realising that everyone in the restaurant was staring at them, Bryony flushed scarlet and tugged Jack's arm.

'For goodness' sake, Jack! Everyone's looking at us.'

Jack gave a dismissive shrug that indicated just how little he was bothered by other people's opinions and then he smiled as his date for the evening joined them. 'Nina, this is David. He's offered to take you home.'

Nina gave Jack a longing look that left no one in any doubt as to how she felt about him. And then she sighed and shot David a dazzling smile. 'If you're sure it's no trouble…'

Wondering why Nina was giving up so easily, Bryony watched as David's eyes dropped to the neckline of Nina's dress which revealed a hypnotic amount of female flesh.

He stared in blatant fascination and then finally cleared his throat and dragged his gaze up to Nina's.

'It's no trouble at all,' he said hoarsely and Bryony resisted the temptation to scream with frustration.

Men were just so pathetic!

Boiling with anger, she said goodnight to David and Nina and followed Jack across the car park.

He unlocked the car and opened the door for her and she slid inside and yanked at the seat belt.

As Jack settled himself in the driver's seat, she let rip.

'David was my date! You had no right to interfere.'

Jack reversed out of his parking space. 'I merely offered to take you home.'

'You didn't offer, Jack,' she said caustically, 'you insisted. David was taking me home and he was ready to argue until your Nina thrust her chest in his face.'

Jack grinned, maddeningly unperturbed by her outburst. 'Impressive, isn't she? I thought as I was taking you away from him, I ought to offer him something in compensation.'

'So I suppose she was the *booby* prize?' Bryony's voice dripped sarcasm and Jack's grin widened.

'Booby prize.' He repeated her words and chuckled with appreciation. 'I admit I hadn't thought of it in exactly those terms, but now you mention it…'

Bryony ground her teeth in frustration. 'You are so hypocritical, do you know that? You have the nerve to criticise my black dress and then you go out with a girl who has a cleavage the size of the Grand Canyon and shows it off to the entire population. I didn't notice you covering *her* up with a coat.'

Jack glanced across at her and in the semi-darkness she could see his eyes twinkling wickedly. 'It would have had to be a big coat and it seemed a shame to deprive everyone of the view,' he drawled, and she felt fury mix with a very different emotion.

Hurt.

When Nina wore a low-cut dress, Jack obviously thought she looked incredibly attractive. But when *she* wore one he thought she looked awful and tried to cover her up.

David had said that she looked nice but, thanks to Jack, David was now with Nina and was doubtless enjoying the view as much as all the other men in the restaurant.

And she was with a man who didn't find her attractive and never would.

'There are times when I hate you, Jack Rothwell,' she muttered, and he gave a soft laugh.

'I don't know what you're getting so worked up about, Blondie.'

For once his use of her nickname irritated her. 'He was my date, Jack. *My date.* And you ruined it.'

To her utter humiliation she felt a lump starting in her throat. She wasn't going to cry in front of Jack.

But fortunately Jack had his eyes fixed on the road. 'How did I ruin it?'

'You really need to ask that question?' She stared at him incredulously. 'I was spending the evening with a man and you suddenly dived in and insisted on taking me home. And I really don't understand why.'

In the moonlight she saw the muscle in his jaw flicker. 'The roads are icy. I didn't want him driving you.'

Her jaw fell open. 'You think you're the only man who can drive on ice?'

'No.' His tone was calm. 'But I've never seen David Armstrong drive on ice and until I do, he's not driving you.'

'Jack, you're being ridiculous!' She looked at him in exasperation. 'And what about Nina? You were perfectly happy for him to drive Nina.'

'Nina can look after herself.'

Bryony slumped back in her seat and gritted her teeth. 'And I can't?'

'You know nothing about men.'

'I thought we were talking about ice?'

'Amongst other things.'

'Oh, right. So we're back to the fact that I haven't dated anyone for ages. It doesn't make me stupid, Jack.'

'And it doesn't make you experienced.'

'Well, it's obvious that I'm never going to get any experience while I'm living in the same town as you!' She glared at him and he gave a shrug.

'I don't know why you're making such a fuss. You had your date. You spent the evening together. Was it good, by the way?'

She opened her mouth to tell him that, no, it had not been good because she'd been staring at him all night, but she realised in time just how much that would reveal about her feelings and stopped herself.

'It was fine,' she lied, 'but it hadn't finished. I wanted *him* to take me home.' And she'd wanted him to kiss her just to see whether it was possible for another man to take her mind off Jack.

'You wanted him to take you home?' There was a tense silence and she saw Jack's fingers tighten on the wheel. 'Why?' His voice was suddenly harsh. 'Or was that where the date was supposed to begin? Keen to make up for lost time, were you?'

His tone was frosty and she gave an exclamation of disgust. 'And so what if it was? What I do with my life is none of your business. I don't need you to look out for me, Jack.'

It was only when he stopped the car and switched off the engine that she realised that they were outside her home. The house was in darkness and suddenly she felt utterly depressed and lonely. Maybe Lizzie was right, she thought miserably. It would be great to walk into her house, knowing that someone was waiting for her. It would be great to have someone to hug her at night. She'd been without a man for almost all her life and suddenly she wanted someone special. Someone who cared whether she came home or not.

But so far her quest for a man had been a disaster.

And suddenly she just wanted to be on her own.

'Well, thanks, Jack. Thanks for ruining my evening.' She undid her seat belt and reached down to pick up her bag. 'I would invite you in for coffee but, seeing as you think that's a euphemism for sex, naturally I wouldn't dream of it. And anyway I'm sure you're dying to get back to Nina.'

'Nina is just a friend.'

'I really couldn't care less, Jack,' she lied, 'because your love life isn't any of my business, just as my love life is none of your business. A whole month has gone past since Lizzie sent her letter to Santa and so far I haven't even managed to get a man to kiss me.'

'You want a man to kiss you?' Jack's voice was a deep growl and without waiting for her answer he slid a hand round her head and brought his mouth down on hers with punishing force. His long fingers bit into her scalp and he lifted his other hand and curved it around her cheek, holding her face still for his kiss.

Utterly shocked, Bryony lifted a hand to his chest, intending to push him away, but instead her traitorous fingers curled into his shirt, then loosened a button and slid inside. Her fingers felt the roughness of his chest hair, warm skin and solid muscle and she felt his grip on her head tighten as his kiss gentled and his tongue traced the seam of her mouth, coaxing her to open for him.

And then he was really kissing her.

Kissing her in the way that she'd always known only he could.

And it felt like magic. How could one person make another feel so different unless it was magic? She was trembling and shivering, overwhelmed by an excitement so intense that she didn't know where it was leading or how it would end. She only knew that she wanted to get closer to him, to crawl all over him but the seats in the car didn't exactly encourage that type of contact. So instead she leaned into him, sliding her hand around his body and trying to draw him closer.

His tongue teased hers gently and then dipped deeper, exploring the interior of her mouth with a lazy expertise that was so erotic it set her entire body on fire. With a maddening degree of self-control, he slid the backs of his fingers over her cheek and down to her neck, trailing his fingers tantalisingly close to her aching breasts before stopping just short of his target. Bryony whimpered with frustration. Longing for his touch, she arched against him but he didn't move his hand. Instead, he continued to kiss her with increasing intensity until none of her senses were under her control.

And then finally, just when she thought her entire body would explode with frustration, he touched her. His strong hand cupped one breast through the silken fabric of her dress and then he drew his thumb over her nipple, creating an agony of sensation so powerful that she gasped against his mouth and shifted in the seat to try and relieve the nagging throb between her thighs.

'Jack…'

The moment she sobbed his name he lifted his head, his breathing unsteady as he stared down at her. Then he released her abruptly and ran a hand over his face, obviously as shaken as she was.

Her whole body screamed in protest that he'd stopped and she looked at him in dazed confusion.

'Jack?'

She saw him tense and then he turned to face her, his handsome face totally blank of expression. 'Now do you see?'

She swallowed, finding it terribly hard to concentrate, still suffering from the aftershocks of his kiss. 'Now do I see what?'

'That kisses can get out of control.' His eyes dropped to her parted lips, still swollen and damp from the ruthless demands of his mouth and then dropped further still to the outline of her breasts which pushed boldly against her dress. He dragged his gaze away and stared into the darkness. 'That's what would have happened if you'd invited David Armstrong back for coffee.'

Bryony stared at him in silence.

She felt as though the world had changed shape. As if everything should look different. It certainly felt different.

For her, their entire relationship had changed in an instant. The moment his mouth had touched hers, everything had become different.

But evidently he didn't feel the same way.

Chewing her lip, she reminded herself that this was Jack. Jack, whose parents had divorced when he was eight and who had vowed never to get married himself when he grew up. And then he'd grown up and had shown no intention of changing his mind about that one fact. Jack didn't do relationships. Judging from the few conversations she'd overheard between her brothers, Jack did sex and not much else.

But even knowing that, her whole body flooded with disappointment as she realised that obviously the kiss hadn't meant anything at all to him. He'd actually been proving a point and in doing so he'd proved something to her, too.

That she'd been right all along about Jack.

He was an amazing kisser.

And she knew that the same thing would never have happened had she invited David Armstrong back for coffee. David might have kissed her, that was true, but she knew that there wasn't another man on the planet who would make her feel what Jack had just made her feel.

But it was totally hopeless.

And the raw, sexual attraction she felt for Jack shouldn't interfere with her determination to find a father for Lizzie, she told herself firmly.

That was just lust and lust always faded anyway.

She needed a man who would be kind, good company and a caring father to Lizzie. She didn't need raw sexual attraction. In fact, raw sexual attraction was starting to turn her into a nervous wreck.

So she lifted her chin and smiled at Jack, proud of how natural it seemed. 'Well, thanks for the practice,' she said lightly, leaning forward and kissing him on the cheek, resisting the almost overwhelming temptation to trace a route to his mouth with the tip of her tongue. 'I'd forgotten how to do it, but you reminded me. Now I know I'll get it right next time I go out with David.'

And with that she opened the door, climbed out of the car and walked to her cottage without looking back.

CHAPTER SIX

DAMN. Damn. Damn.

What the hell had he done?

He'd kissed his best friend.

Jack stared after Bryony, trying to decide what shocked him most. The fact that he'd kissed her, or the fact that he hadn't wanted to stop.

He sat in the car with the engine switched off, staring into the frozen darkness feeling as though something fundamental to his existence had changed.

Where had it come from? That sudden impulse to kiss her...

Blondie was family.

As much a baby sister to him as she was to Tom and Oliver.

And until tonight he'd never thought of her in any other way.

Or had he?

Had he really never thought of her like that or was it just that he'd trained himself not to?

He sat still, watching the house, and then suddenly the lights went on. He saw her walk into her cosy sitting room and shrug off her coat, revealing that amazing red dress and an avalanche of blonde hair.

For years he hadn't seen her in a dress and suddenly she seemed to be wearing a different one every week.

He closed his eyes and breathed deeply, still able

to detect the tantalising scent of her hair and skin. The instantaneous reaction of his body was so powerful that he gritted his teeth and shifted slightly in his seat, trying to find a more comfortable position.

There wasn't one.

Suddenly, somehow, she'd invaded every part of him.

He'd made an unconscious decision never to cross that boundary but now he'd crossed it there was no going back.

Whichever way he looked at her, he didn't see a surrogate sister any more. And he didn't see his best friend. He saw a woman. A living, breathing, stunningly beautiful woman.

But he couldn't do anything about it.

Lizzie was looking for a father. Someone strong who could swing her in the garden. Someone funny who'd let her watch television before school and who wouldn't make her eat sprouts.

Well, he could do that bit with no problem. He wasn't that keen on sprouts himself so he was more than happy to collude over their exclusion from their diet. And he had no trouble swinging her in the garden, hugging her and making her laugh. In fact, he was great at all those things.

The problem came with the last bit of her letter.

I want a daddy who will hug my mummy and stay with us for ever.

Jack leaned his head back against the seat and let out a long breath. He didn't do for ever. He had trouble doing next month. The whole concept of 'for ever' frightened the life out of him.

And Bryony knew that.

She knew him better than anyone.

Which was probably why she'd looked so shocked when he'd kissed her. Hell, *he'd* been shocked! And now he was confused, too, which was a totally new experience for him. He was *never* confused about women. He knew *exactly* what he wanted from them.

Everything, as long as it wasn't permanent.

Which meant that he had absolutely nothing to offer Bryony.

He started the engine and clenched his hands on the wheel. *He had to stop noticing her as a woman.* Surely it couldn't be that hard? After all, he'd only just started noticing her that way. It couldn't be that hard to go back to seeing her as his best friend.

He'd just carry on as they always had. Dropping round to see her. Chatting in her kitchen. And seeing other women.

It would be fine.

If working with Jack had been hard before the kiss, for Bryony it became even harder afterwards.

When he walked into a room she knew instantly, even when she had her back to him.

She didn't need to see him. She *felt* him. Felt his presence with every feminine bone in her body.

And she noticed everything about him. The way the solid muscle of his shoulders moved when he reached up to yank an X-ray out of the lightbox, the way his head tilted slightly when he was concentrating on something and the way everyone always asked his opinion on everything. She noticed how good he was with anxious relatives, how strong and capable he was with terrified patients and how well he dealt with inexperienced staff. He was the cleverest doctor she'd ever worked with and he had an instinctive feel for what was wrong with a patient before he'd even examined them.

If she'd had butterflies before he'd kissed her, they seemed to have multiplied since the kiss.

Which was utterly ridiculous because obviously, for him, nothing had changed.

Their relationship followed the same pattern of blonde jokes, man jokes and evenings when he sat with his feet on her table in the kitchen, watching while she cooked, a bottle of beer snuggled in his lap.

And now they were into December and there was no sign of a man who was even remotely close to fulfilling Lizzie's criteria for a daddy.

David hadn't asked her out again and she'd resigned herself to the fact that he was probably now dating Nina.

'Are you upset about that?' she asked Jack one evening, when they were curled up in front of the fire. She was writing Christmas cards and he was staring into the flames with a distant look in his eyes.

'Upset about what?'

'Nina.' She said the other woman's name as lightly as possible. 'Someone told me that she's seeing David Armstrong.'

'Is she?' Jack suppressed a yawn and stretched long legs out in front of him. 'Well, good for him.'

'You never should have sent them home together. I'm amazed you're not upset.'

He gave her a mocking smile. 'Come on, Blondie. How long have you known me?'

She stared at him. 'You engineered it, didn't you?'

Her pen fell to the floor as she suddenly realised what had happened. 'You got rid of her.'

His gaze didn't flicker. 'I encouraged her to find someone else, yes.'

'Why?' Bryony shook her head, puzzled. 'She was nice. And she seemed crazy about you.'

Jack looked at her steadily. 'She was.'

Which was why he'd ended it.

It was Jack's usual pattern.

Bryony sighed. 'Jack, you're thirty-four,' she said softly. 'You can't run for ever.'

He gave a funny lopsided grin that made her heart turn over. 'Watch me.'

'Listen…' She put her pen down and gave up on her Christmas cards. They could wait. 'I know your parents' divorce was really difficult for you, but you can't—'

'Drop it, Blondie. I don't want to talk about it.' His eyes glittered ominously and she saw the warning in the blue depths. Taboo subject.

She sighed. 'But, Jack, you can't—'

'Why did the blonde tiptoe past the medicine cabinet?' he drawled lazily, and she rolled her eyes, exasperated by his refusal to talk about his emotions.

'I don't know.'

'Because she didn't want to wake the sleeping pills.' Jack gave a wicked smile that made her heart jump in her chest.

He was so shockingly handsome it was totally unfair, and when he smiled like that she just melted.

'How many men does it take to change a toilet roll?' She smiled sweetly. 'No one knows. It's never been done. So what did Nina do wrong?'

Jack gave a sardonic smile. 'Frankly? She said, "I love you",' he said dryly, and gave a mock shudder. 'Which is the same as "goodbye" in my language.'

Bryony rolled her eyes. 'They always say that if you want to get rid of a man, you should say "I love you, I want to marry you and most of all I want to have your children." It's guaranteed to leave skid marks.'

Jack laughed. 'That's just about the size of it. Why do you think I bought a Ferrari?'

Bryony sighed. 'Poor Nina.'

'She knew the score.'

But Bryony was willing to bet that knowing the score hadn't made it any easier. On the other hand, Nina seemed to have moved on quite happily to David so she couldn't have been that broken-hearted.

'One day you'll settle down, Jack,' Bryony predicted, licking another envelope. 'You'll be such a great father.'

'That's nonsense.'

'Look how great you are with Lizzie.'

'That's because I have all the fun and none of the responsibility,' he said shortly, frowning slightly as he looked at her.

'I don't think that's true. Lizzie expects a lot from you and you always deliver. How many netball matches have you been to this year?'

Jack grinned. 'Lots. You know me. Rugby, rock-climbing, netball—my three favourite sports.'

She laughed. 'Precisely. The sight of you standing on the side of a netball court would be funny if it wasn't so touching.' She added the envelope to the ever-growing pile. 'And it is touching, Jack. You're fantastic with Lizzie.'

A muscle worked in his jaw. 'But what she really wants is a father.'

Bryony shrugged. 'And who can blame her for that?'

'She doesn't realise that fathers aren't perfect.'

'I think she probably does, actually. But she still wants someone.'

'So how is the quest going? Any suitable candidates lined up? Obviously David is now off the scene…'

Something in his tone made her glance up at him but his expression was neutral.

'Well, it's not going that well,' Bryony muttered, licking another envelope and adding it to the pile. 'Christmas is three weeks away and I don't have another date until Saturday.'

His expression was suddenly hostile. 'You have a date on Saturday? Who with?'

Bryony blushed slightly. 'Toby.'

'Toby who?' Jack was frowning and she laughed.

'You know—our Toby. Toby from the mountain rescue team.'

'You're kidding!' He glared at her. 'Toby? He's totally unsuitable.'

'Calm down, Jack,' Bryony said mildly, gathering up all the envelopes and putting them on the table. 'Toby is nice. And he's always been kind to Lizzie.'

'Toby has a terrible reputation with women,' Jack said frostily, and she shrugged.

'So do you, Jack.'

'But I'm not dating you.'

And how she wished he was. Her gaze met his and held and then he sucked in a breath and rose to his feet, powerful and athletic.

'You can't date Toby.'

'Why not?'

There was a long silence and a muscle twitched in his jaw. 'Because he isn't right for you.'

She sighed. 'Jack, you're so jaded about relationships that you're never going to think anyone is right, but trust me when I say I'm not going to choose anyone who would hurt Lizzie.'

He took several deep breaths. 'I don't want anyone to hurt you either.'

'I know that.' She smiled at him, touched that he cared at least that much. 'You don't need to be so protective. It's nice, but I can look after myself.'

'Where are you going on Saturday?'

She wondered why he was asking and then decided that it was idle curiosity. 'Actually, I don't know. Toby is keeping it a secret.' She smiled. 'Isn't it romantic?'

'Suspicious is the word I would use,' Jack muttered, grabbing his coat and car keys and making for the door. 'I'll talk to him.'

Bryony gave an exasperated sigh. 'Jack, you are not my minder.'

'Toby is definitely not to be trusted when it comes to women,' Jack growled. 'I want him to know that I'm looking out for you.'

'I should think he knows that, seeing as you spend half your life in my house,' Bryony pointed out mildly, and he nodded.

'Well, let's hope so. I won't have him messing either of my girls around.'

His girls.

Bryony swallowed and her eyes clashed with his. Something flickered in those blue depths and she knew that he was remembering their kiss. 'We're not "your girls", Jack.'

He hesitated and a strange expression crossed his handsome face as he stared down at her. Then he muttered something under his breath, jerked open the front door and left the house.

The next day the temperature dropped further still and it started to snow. Wrapped up in her MRT gear, Bryony was posting her Christmas cards when her pager went off.

Relieved that Lizzie was spending the day with her mother, she drove herself to the rescue base, which was less than five minutes' drive from her house.

'Two women out walking,' Jack told her, zipping up his jacket. 'One has cut herself and one has an ankle injury.' He exchanged looks with Bryony. 'What is it with women and ankles?'

'I don't know but at least it gives you and me an excuse to climb mountains in filthy weather,' she said happily, and he smiled.

'I suppose there is that.'

The rest of the team gathered, picking up equipment and listening while they were given a brief.

'We're not sure where they are—' Sean, leader of the MRT, tapped a point on the map '—but this was where they were aiming for when it started to snow. The path is covered now and they're totally lost.'

Bryony looked at the map. 'It's really easy to lose that path in bad weather,' she said. 'I know because I've done it myself.'

Jack rolled his eyes. 'Never let a blonde loose on a mountain,' he drawled, but his eyes gleamed wickedly and she smiled back at him.

'At least a girl will ask for directions if she's lost. Men never ask for directions.'

'That's because they don't need to. Men don't get lost,' Jack returned blithely, and Sean sighed.

'Maybe you two could argue on the way,' he suggested mildly, pointing at the map. 'Ben, you go with Toby up this path and hopefully we'll come across them. Stay in touch. And watch yourselves. The weather is awful. I'll deploy the rest of the team as they arrive.'

Toby glanced at Bryony. 'I could go with Bryony…'

'No, you couldn't.' Jack's response was instantaneous, his blue gaze hard and uncompromising. 'I go with Bryony.'

Toby's eyes narrowed slightly and then he shrugged. 'Whatever.'

Bryony followed Jack out of the rescue base and they drove a short distance and parked the four-wheel-drive in a farm near the path.

Jack hoisted the rucksack onto his back and waited while she did the same thing. 'Come on. We need to get going before we freeze to death.'

They set off at a brisk pace and she glanced at the sky. 'It's going to snow again in a minute.'

'It's Christmas,' Jack pointed out. 'It's supposed to snow.'

Bryony gave a shiver and pulled her fleece up to her chin. 'Well, it looks nice on the Christmas cards but it's not so great when you're out on the mountains. Why didn't you let me go with Toby?'

'Because he'd be so busy staring at your legs he'd let you fall down a crevice.'

Bryony gaped at him. 'Jack, I'm wearing fleece trousers. They're hardly revealing!'

'Your legs would look sexy in a bin bag.'

She stopped dead. He thought her legs were sexy? He'd never said anything like that to her before. She was staring after him in confusion, wondering why he'd said that, when he glanced back at her.

'Why have you stopped? You needed to admire me from a distance?'

She grinned, suddenly feeling light-hearted. 'Why are men like placemats?' Shifting her rucksack slightly to make it more comfortable, she caught up with him. 'Because they only show up when there's food on the table.'

He smiled and as they continued up the path it started to snow again. 'I hope they've got some form of shelter,' Jack muttered, and Bryony nodded, her expression concerned.

'I hope we find them soon. It'll be dark in a couple of hours.'

They trudged on and the snow suddenly grew thicker underfoot.

'Crampons and ice axes, I think, Blondie,' Jack muttered, pausing by a snow-covered rock and swinging his rucksack off his back.

They stopped just long enough to equip themselves

safely for the next part of the rescue and then they were off again.

Bryony stayed behind Jack, watching him place his feet firmly and confidently in the snow, the sharp points of his crampons biting into the snow.

They walked for what felt like ages and then suddenly heard shouts from above them.

'Sounds hopeful,' Jack said, increasing his pace and altering his direction slightly. 'We'll check it out and then I'll radio in to base.'

Bryony breathed a sigh of relief when they rounded the next corner and saw two women huddled together.

'Watch your footing here,' Jack said, frowning slightly as he glanced to his right. 'There's a slope there and a sheer drop at the end of it. I know because I climbed up that rockface last summer with your brothers. This snow doesn't feel very stable to me.'

'Shall we rope up?'

He shook his head. 'We're all right for now, but we'll rope up before we go down.'

They reached the two women and one of them immediately burst into tears.

'Oh, thank goodness…'

Bryony dropped onto her knees beside her, aware that Jack was already on the radio, giving their exact location to the rest of the team.

'You're going to be fine,' she said gently, slipping her arm around the woman's shoulders and giving her a hug. 'Where are you hurt?'

'I'm not hurt,' the woman said, but her teeth were chattering and she was obviously very cold. 'But my sister slipped on the snow and hurt her ankle and cut her wrist. I think she must have hit a rock when she landed. It was bleeding very badly so I pressed on it hard with a spare jumper that we had in our bag and it seemed to stop.'

'Good—you did just the right thing.' Bryony shrugged her rucksack off her back. 'I'm Bryony and I'm a doctor and a member of the local mountain rescue team. What's your name?'

'Alison Gayle.' The woman was shivering. 'And my sister's name is Pamela. I feel so guilty dragging you out in this weather. We've put everyone in danger.'

'Don't feel guilty,' Bryony said immediately, 'and you haven't put us in danger. It's our job and we love it. And we have all the right equipment for this weather.'

Which was just as well, she reflected ruefully, because the weather was getting worse by the second.

The snow started to fall heavily and Bryony brushed the soft flakes away from her face with a gloved hand and looked at the sky with a frown. The visibility was reducing rapidly. She moved over to check on Pamela and Jack joined her.

'All right, the rest of the team is on their way up.' He dropped down next to her and smiled at Alison. 'Lovely day for a stroll in the hills.'

Bryony moved over to Pamela and noticed that the woman looked extremely pale and shocked.

'You're going to be fine now, Pamela,' she said firmly. 'I'm just going to check your injuries and then we're going to get you off this mountain.'

She pulled off her gloves and carefully unwrapped the blood-soaked jumper so that she could examine the wrist injury more carefully. As soon as she released the pressure and exposed the wound, blood spurted into the air and Bryony quickly grabbed the jumper and pressed down again.

'It's an artery, Jack,' she muttered and he was by her side in an instant, the bulk of his shoulders providing a barrier between her and the elements.

He was strong and confident and, as usual, she found his presence hugely reassuring.

'I've put Alison into a casualty bag so she'll be fine for the time being.' He unwrapped the wrist himself, quickly assessed the extent of the injury and then pressed a sterile pad over the laceration and smiled at Pamela.

'That's going to be fine,' he said smoothly, elevating her arm and handing a bandage to Bryony with his free hand. 'We're going to bandage it tightly and keep it up just until we can get you off this mountain.'

The woman looked at him with frightened eyes. 'I can't walk down—my ankle hurts.'

'Don't you worry about that. That's why we bring my blonde friend here,' Jack said cheerfully, winking at Bryony. 'She's the muscles of the operation.'

While he chatted and teased, Bryony tightened the bandage and gave him a nod. 'All done.'

'Good. So now let's check the ankle. How painful is it, Pamela?'

The woman looked at him, her lips turning blue with the cold. 'Agony.'

'So we'll give you some gas and air to breathe while we check it out,' Jack said immediately, reaching into his rucksack. 'I want you to take some slow breaths. Great—perfect.' He looked at Bryony. 'Right, can you cut that boot off and let's see what we're dealing with here? And make it quick. She's cold and we need to get her into a casualty bag.'

Bryony sliced through the laces and gently removed the boot and then the sock. 'The ankle is very swollen,' she murmured, and Pamela gave a little groan and took several more breaths of the gas and air. 'Could you put any weight on it after you fell, Pamela?'

The woman shook her head. 'It was agony. I fell straight away, that's how I cut my wrist.'

'What do you reckon, Blondie?' Jack asked, his arm around Pamela as he supported her.

'She's tender over the distal fibula and the lateral malleolus,' Bryony said quickly. 'I think it's probably a fracture. She's going to need X-rays when we get her down.'

'So we splint it now, give her some more analgesia and then get her into a casualty bag until the rest of the team gets here with the Bell,' Jack said decisively, his arm still round Pamela. 'You're going to be fine, Pamela.'

Pamela groaned. 'Have I broken it? And why do you need a bell?'

'A Bell is a type of stretcher that we use, and it looks as though you might have broken your ankle,' Jack said, watching as Bryony pulled out the rest of the equipment. 'Don't you worry. We're going to make you comfortable. We have these amazing fleecy bags that are very snug. In a moment you're going to feel like toast. Did you hear about the blonde who ordered a take-away pizza? The waiter asked her if she wanted it cut into six slices or twelve—' swiftly he helped Bryony apply the splint '—and she said, "Six, please. I could never eat twelve."'

'Just ignore him, Pamela,' Bryony advised with a smile. 'He doesn't know the meaning of politically correct and frankly it's amazing he hasn't been arrested before now. If I didn't need him to carry you down this mountain, I'd push him off the cliff myself.'

But despite the pain she was obviously suffering, Pamela was smiling. 'He's making me laugh, actually.'

Bryony groaned. 'Don't tell him that or he'll tell you blonde jokes all the way down the mountain. Trust me, you'd rather be left on your own in the snow than have to listen to Jack in full flow.'

She and Jack kept up their banter, taking Pamela's mind off the situation she was in, working together with swift efficiency. They'd just got Pamela into a casualty bag when the rest of the team approached out of the snow. Bryony's brother was among them.

Jack rolled his eyes. 'The last thing we need up here is an obstetrician,' he drawled. 'Who's delivering all those babies while you're wasting your time on the mountain?'

Tom adjusted the pack on his back. 'They're all queuing up, waiting for me to come back.'

'Well, you took so long you needn't have bothered coming.' Jack stood up, tall and broad-shouldered. 'You've missed all the action. Blondie and I have sorted it out as usual. Don't know why we need such a big team really.'

'If we weren't here you wouldn't have anyone to boss around,' Tom said dryly, working with the rest of the team to get a stretcher ready. 'We rang the RAF to see if there was any chance of an airlift but the weather is closing in so it looks like we're going to have to carry them down.'

Jack walked over and conferred with Sean, the other A and E consultant and the MRT leader, and discussed the best way to get the two women off the mountain while Bryony kept an eye on Pamela. Fortunately the casualty bag had zip access, which meant she was able to check on her patient without exposing her to the freezing air.

Finally Pamela was safely strapped onto a stretcher. Her sister had revived sufficiently to be able to walk down the mountain with some assistance from two bulky MRT members who roped her between them.

Bryony reattached her crampons and picked up her ice axe. The snow was thick now and she knew that one false step could have her sliding halfway down the mountain.

The snow was falling so thickly she could barely see and she scrubbed her face with her hand to clear her vision.

'Rope up, Blondie,' Jack's voice said, and as she opened her mouth to answer, the ground beneath her suddenly shifted and she was falling.

She didn't even have time to cry out, sliding fast down the slope towards the edge of the cliff that Jack had described so graphically.

Immediately she braced the axe shaft across her body, digging the pick into the snow slope and raising her feet so that they didn't catch in the snow. She jerked to a halt and hung there for a moment, suspended, her heart hammering against her chest, her hands tightly locked on her ice axe, which was the only thing holding her on the slope.

She heard Jack calling her name and heard something in his tone that she hadn't heard before. Panic.

She closed her eyes briefly and took a deep breath. She didn't want Jack to panic. Jack never panicked. Ever. Jack panicking was a bad sign. Realising just how close she was to the edge of the cliff, she kept a tight hold on her ice axe and gingerly moved her feet, trying to get some traction with her crampons.

'Hang on, Bry,' Tom called cheerfully. 'Jack's just coming to get you. You won't live this one down in a hurry.'

But despite his light-hearted tone, Bryony heard the anxiety in his voice. And it was hardly surprising, she thought ruefully, risking another glance below her. Another couple of metres and she would have vanished over the edge of a sheer cliff.

And it could still happen.

'Hang on, Blondie,' Jack called, and she glanced up to see him climbing down towards her, a rope attached to his middle.

'You think I'm going to let go?' Her voice shook slightly. 'You think I'm that stupid?'

As he drew closer she could see his grin. 'Of course you're stupid. You fell, didn't you? And you have blonde hair. You must be stupid. It says so in all the books.'

Bryony tried to smile but then she felt the snow give under her ice axe and she gave a gasp of fright and jabbed her feet into the slope. *'Jack!'*

'I've got you, angel.' His voice came from right beside her and he slid an arm and leg over her, holding her against the slope while he attached a rope to her waist. 'God, you almost gave us all a heart attack.'

She turned her head to look at him and his face was so close that she could feel the warmth of his breath against her cheek and see the dark stubble shadowing his hard jaw. He looked sexy and strong and she'd never been so pleased to see anyone in her life.

Then she glanced down at the drop beneath her and thought of Lizzie. 'Oh, God, Jack,' she whispered, and she felt his grip on her tighten.

'Don't even say it,' he said harshly. 'I've got you and there's no way I'm letting you go.' He glanced up the slope and shouted something to Sean, who was holding the other end of the rope. 'They're going to take you up now, sweetheart. Try not to do anything blonde on the way up.'

She gave a weak smile and he smiled back. 'Go for it.'

And gradually, with the aid of the rope and her ice axe and crampons, she managed to climb back up the slope, aware that Jack was behind her.

Finally she reached the top and Tom rolled his eyes. 'Thanks for the adrenaline rush.'

'Any time,' Bryony said lightly, but she was shaking badly now that the danger had passed, and Jack must have known that because he pulled her into his arms and held her until his warmth and strength gradually calmed her.

He didn't speak. He just held her tightly, talking all the time to Sean and Tom as they reassessed the best way to get safely down the increasingly treacherous slope.

Bryony stood in the circle of his arms, wishing that she could stay there for ever. There was no better place in the world, she decided, closing her eyes and breathing in his tantalising male scent.

And when he finally released her she felt bereft.

She looked at him, trying to keep it light as he checked the rope at her waist. 'I didn't know you were into bondage.'

He smiled down at her as he pulled on the rope. 'There's a lot you don't know about me, Blondie,' he drawled, his blue eyes teasing her wickedly. 'There's no point in learning to do all these fancy knots if you don't put them to good use.'

She smiled and then her smile faltered. 'Thanks, Jack.' Ridiculously she felt close to tears. 'I would have done the same for you.'

He winked at her, maddeningly self-confident. 'I wouldn't have fallen, babe.'

She gasped in outrage. 'You arrogant…!' Words failed her and he smiled and flicked her cheek with a gloved finger.

'That's better. At least you've got your colour back. Let's get moving.'

He turned to Sean and she realised that his inflammatory statement had been a ploy to rouse her to anger. Which meant he must have guessed how close she'd been to tears.

She gave a reluctant laugh, acknowledging once more just how clever he was.

It was much easier to get down the mountain feeling annoyed and irritated than it was feeling scared and tearful.

In the end it took several hours to get down safely

and the two women were immediately transferred to A and E in the MRT ambulance.

Jack drove Bryony home, the swirling snow falling thickly on the windscreen. 'If this carries on we're going to be busy in A and E,' he said, his eyes searching as he glanced at her.

'I'm OK.'

He nodded. 'Thanks to your ice axe technique. You did well. That's if you overlook the fact that you fell in the first place.'

She gaped at him. 'I did not fall,' she protested. 'The mountain slipped out from beneath me.'

'It wasn't my fault I crashed the car, Officer,' Jack said, mimicking her tone. 'The road suddenly moved.'

Bryony pulled a face. 'What's it like being so damn perfect, Jack?'

'I've learned to live with it,' he said solemnly, 'but I realise it's tough on those who struggle around me.'

'You can say that again,' she muttered darkly, dragging off her hat and scraping her hair back from her face. 'One of these days I'm probably going to shoot you.'

'Is that before or after I save you from falling over a cliff?'

She groaned. 'You're never going to let me forget that, are you?'

'Probably not.' He pulled up outside her house and switched the engine off. 'So are you going to invite me to supper tomorrow night?'

There was a gleam in his eyes and she felt butterflies flicker inside her stomach. 'I have a date with Toby,' she croaked, and his eyes narrowed slightly.

'Of course you have.' He was silent for a moment and then he smiled. 'Another time, then.'

He leaned across to open the car door for her and she fought against the temptation to lean forward and hug him. He was so close—and so male…

Suddenly she wished she didn't have the date with Toby. She would rather have spent an evening with Jack.

But then she remembered Lizzie's Christmas list. She shouldn't be spending her evenings with Jack. It was a waste of time.

'Lizzie and I are going to choose our Christmas tree tomorrow,' she said, telling herself that spending time with Jack during the day didn't count. 'Do you want to come? She'd love you to join us, I know she would.'

Jack grinned. 'Will I have to play Weddings?'

'Probably, but you're getting very good at it now so I don't see the problem.'

'All right, I'd like to come.'

'Goodnight, then, Jack,' she said softly, undoing her seat belt and gathering up her stuff. 'I'll see you tomorrow.'

And she scrambled out of the car without looking back.

CHAPTER SEVEN

'I WANT the biggest tree in the forest.' Lizzie clapped her hands together and beamed at Jack, her breath clouding the freezing air. She was wearing pink fleecy trousers tucked into pink fleecy boots, a bright, stripy scarf wrapped round her neck, and she was bursting with excitement. 'The tree has to be big if Santa is going to fit my present under it.'

Bryony chewed her lip and exchanged glances with Jack. 'You know, sweetheart,' she said anxiously, 'I'm not sure we gave Santa enough notice to find a daddy. That's a pretty big present.'

'He'll manage it,' Lizzie said happily, stamping her feet to keep warm, 'because I've been extra good. Sally stole my gloves in the playground and I didn't even tell.'

Jack frowned. 'Someone stole your gloves?'

'They were new and she liked them.'

Jack looked at Bryony. 'Another child stole her gloves?'

'It's fine, Jack,' Bryony said hastily, knowing just how protective Jack could be of Lizzie. 'She'll sort it out.'

'You should speak to her teacher.'

'*It's fine, Jack!*' Bryony shot him a warning look. 'Now, let's go and choose this tree, shall we?'

Jack sucked in a breath and smiled. 'Good idea.' He took Lizzie's hand in his. 'We'll get you some new gloves, peanut. Any pair you want. We'll choose them together.'

They walked amongst the trees and Lizzie sprinted up to one and tilted her head back, gazing up in awe.

'I like *this* one.'

Bryony looked at it in dismay. 'Lizzie, it's the tallest tree here!'

'I know.' Lizzie stroked the branches lovingly, watching as the needles sprang back. 'I love it. It's big. Like having the whole forest in your house. And I like the way it smells.' She leaned forward and breathed in and Bryony sighed.

'It won't fit into our living room, sweetheart. How about that one over there—it's a lovely shape.'

Lizzie shook her head, her hand still locked around one branch of the tree she'd chosen as if she couldn't quite let it go. 'I love this one. I want this to be our tree.'

Bryony closed her eyes briefly. 'Lizzie—'

'It's a great tree and we can always trim the top,' Jack said firmly, and Bryony lifted an eyebrow.

'You're planning to lop six feet off the top?'

He grinned. 'If need be.' He squatted down next to Lizzie, his hair shining glossily black next to the little girl's blonde curls. 'The lady likes this one. So the lady gets this one.'

'You need to learn to say no to her, Jack.'

'Why would I want to say no?' He scooped Lizzie into his arms and grinned at her. 'So you want this tree?'

Lizzie nodded and slipped her arm round his neck. 'Can I have it?'

'Of course.' Still holding the child, Jack slipped a

hand into his pocket and removed his wallet. 'Here we are, Blondie. Merry Christmas.'

Bryony shook her head. 'I'll pay, Jack.'

'My treat.' His eyes locked on hers, his expression warm. 'Please.'

She hesitated and then smiled. 'All right. Thanks.'

Lizzie tightened her arms round Jack's neck. 'Why do you call Mummy Blondie?'

'Because she has blonde hair, of course.'

'But I have blonde hair, too.'

Jack gave a start. 'So you do! Goodness—I never noticed.'

Lizzie gave a delicious chuckle. 'Yes, you did. I know you're joking.' She hugged him tight and then looked at him thoughtfully. 'Jack…'

His eyes narrowed. 'Don't tell me, you want to go home and play Weddings?'

'No.' She lifted a small hand and touched his cheek. 'I asked Santa for a daddy for Christmas.'

Jack went still. 'I know you did.'

'Well, now I wish I'd asked him to make you my daddy,' Lizzie said wistfully. 'I love you, Jack. No one plays Weddings like you do.'

Bryony swallowed hard, the lump in her throat so big it threatened to choke her.

'Lizzie…' Jack's voice sounded strangely thick and his hard jaw was tense as he struggled to find the right words. 'I can't be your daddy, sweetheart. But I'll always be here for you.'

'Why can't you be my daddy? I know Mummy loves you.'

Bryony closed her eyes, fire in her cheeks, but Jack just gave a strange-sounding laugh.

'And I love your mummy. But not in the way that mummies and daddies are supposed to love each other.'

Bryony rubbed her booted foot in the snow and wished an avalanche would consume her. But there wasn't much chance of that in the forest. So instead she looked up and gave a bright smile.

'But Santa is going to choose you a great present,' she said brightly. 'I know he is, and in the meantime we'd better buy this super-special tree before anyone else does. It's the best one in the forest and I can see other people looking at it.'

Lizzie's eyes widened in panic. 'Hurry up, then!'

Bryony took Jack's wallet and went to pay while he opened the boot of the four-wheel-drive and manoeuvred the huge tree inside, with Lizzie jumping up and down next to him.

'Most of the needles have just landed on the inside of the vehicle,' he muttered to Bryony as they climbed into the front and strapped Lizzie in. 'I think we might be decorating twigs when we get it home.'

Bryony glanced at him, wondering if he realised that he'd called her house 'home'.

'Are you getting a tree yourself, Jack?' she asked, and he shook his head, holding the wheel firmly as he negotiated the rutted track that led out of the forest onto the main road.

'What's the point? I'm going to be working for most of it.' He glanced at Lizzie who was listening to a tape through her headphones and not paying any attention. 'And, anyway, Christmas is for children.'

Bryony gave him a searching look. 'Are you coming to Mum's this year?'

Jack concentrated on the road. 'I don't know. Sean wants to be with Ally and the kids so I've said I'll work.'

'You come every year, Jack.' Bryony frowned. 'Lizzie would be so disappointed if you weren't there. All of us would. You're part of our family. At least come for part of it.'

'Maybe.' His shrug was noncommittal and she sighed.

'I know Christmas isn't your favourite time of year.'

There was a long silence and then he sucked in a breath, his eyes still on the road. 'Christmas is for families, Blondie. I don't have one.'

Bryony bit her lip. 'Have you heard from your mother lately?'

'A postcard six months ago.' He turned the wheel to avoid a hole in the road. 'She's with her latest lover in Brazil.'

Bryony was silent and he turned to look at her, a mocking look in his eyes. 'Don't feel sorry for me. I'm thirty-four. I certainly don't expect my mother to come home and play happy families after all this time. I think that's one game we never mastered in our house. When everyone else was unwrapping presents around the tree, my parents were at different ends of the house nurturing grievances.'

'Jack—'

'And that was a good thing.' He gave a grim smile. 'If they ever met the rows were so bad I used to run and hide in the garden. Once I was out there all night and they didn't even notice. I always used to think that was why we had such a big house with so much land. Because no one wanted to live next door to anyone who argued as much as my parents.'

His experience was such a contrast to her own happy childhood that Bryony felt suddenly choked.

'You used to come to us.'

'Yeah.' He gave a funny smile. 'You were the perfect family.'

Bryony looked at him, suddenly wondering for the first time whether that had made it worse for him. 'Was it hard for you, being with us?'

He shook his head. 'It wasn't hard, Blondie. You always made me feel as though I was Santa himself from the moment I walked through the door. How could that be hard?'

Bryony smiled. She used to stand with her nose pressed against the window, waiting for Jack to arrive. Longing to show him her presents.

'You were just like Lizzie.' His voice softened at the memory. 'I remember the year you had your ballet dress from Santa. You wore it with your Wellington boots because you were dying to play outside in the snow but no one could persuade you to take it off. You were in the garden building a snowman in pink satin and tulle. Do you remember?'

'I remember tearing it climbing a tree.' Bryony laughed. 'I just wanted to keep up with my brothers.'

On impulse she reached out and touched his leg, feeling the rock-hard muscle under her fingers. 'Come for Christmas, Jack. Please?'

He gave her a funny, lopsided smile that was so sexy she suddenly found it hard to breathe. 'Better see what Santa produces for Lizzie first,' he said softly, turning into the road that led to her cottage. 'I might not be welcome.'

Bryony slumped back in her seat, the reminder that she'd so far failed to solve the problem of Lizzie's Christmas present bursting her bubble of happiness.

What was she going to do about Lizzie's present?

At some point soon she was going to have to sit her little girl down and tell her that Santa couldn't deliver a daddy. Otherwise Christmas morning was going to be a disappointment.

Trying to console herself with the thought that there must be something else that Lizzie would like for Christmas, Bryony realised that Jack had stopped the car.

'Ready to unload this tree?' He glanced behind him and winced. 'I can't believe you chose a tree that big.'

Lizzie pulled the headphones off her ears and giggled. 'It wasn't Mummy, it was you, Jack.'

'Me?' He looked horrified as he jumped out of the car with athletic grace and turned to lift the little girl out. 'I chose that?'

Lizzie was laughing. 'You know you did.'

'Well, we'd better get it in your house, then.'

Laughing and grumbling, Jack dragged the tree inside the house and proceeded to secure it in a bucket with his usual calm efficiency.

Bryony gazed upwards and shook her head in disbelief. 'It's bent at the top.'

'It's perfect,' Lizzie sighed, and Jack nodded solemnly.

'Perfect.'

Bryony rolled her eyes, forced to accept that she

was outnumbered. 'OK. Well, we've got it now, so let's decorate it.'

They spent the rest of the afternoon draping the tree with lights and baubles until it sparkled festively. Lizzie produced a pink fairy to go on top of the tree and Jack lifted her so that she could position it herself.

Then Jack went into the garden and cut boughs of holly from the tree and they decorated the fireplace.

Bryony produced mince pies and they sat on the carpet, admiring their decorations and enjoying the atmosphere.

Bryony smiled as she looked around her. 'I feel Christmassy.'

'That's because of the size of the tree,' Jack told her, his handsome face serious as he bit into a mince pie. 'Any smaller and you wouldn't be feeling the way you're feeling now.'

But watching him and Lizzie fighting over the last mince pie, Bryony realised that the warm Christmassy feeling that she had in the pit of her stomach had nothing to do with the tree and everything to do with the three of them being together. They felt like a family.

But they weren't a family.

Jack didn't want to be part of a family.

Watching Lizzie climbing all over him, dropping crumbs over his trousers and the carpet, Bryony wondered if he realised that he actually *was* part of a family.

Whether he liked it or not, he was a huge part of her life. And she couldn't imagine it any other way, even if ultimately she found a daddy for Lizzie. And just thinking of how she was going to tell Lizzie that Santa hadn't managed to produce a daddy on Christmas Day filled her with overwhelming depression.

Suddenly needing to be on her own, Bryony stood up. 'I need to get ready. Toby's picking me up at seven,' she said brightly, 'and I don't want to smell like a Christmas tree.'

She half expected Jack to say something about her going out with Toby. After all, he'd been less than enthusiastic about her other attempts to date men. But he just smiled at her and carried on playing with Lizzie.

Feeling deflated and not really understanding why, Bryony ran herself a deep bath and lay in a nest of scented bubbles for half an hour, telling herself that she was going to have a really great evening with Toby.

She was going to wear the black dress again.

And it was nothing to do with Jack's comments about her having good legs, she told herself firmly as she dried herself and dressed carefully. It was just that the dress suited her and she knew that Toby was planning to take her somewhere special.

She spent time on her make-up and pinned her hair on top of her head in a style that she felt suited the dress.

Finally satisfied, she walked out of her bedroom and into the kitchen, where Jack was making Lizzie tea and playing a game of 'guess the animal'.

'You're a tiger, Jack.' Lizzie giggled, watching with delight as he prowled around the kitchen, growling. 'Do I have to eat sprouts? I hate sprouts. Can I have peas instead?'

'Never argue with a tiger,' Jack said sternly, putting two sprouts on the side of her plate. 'Eat up. They're good for you.'

Lizzie stared at them gloomily. 'I hate things that are good for me.'

'He's only given you two,' Bryony said mildly, turning to lift two mugs out of the cupboard. When she looked back the sprouts had gone. Lizzie and Jack were both concentrating hard on the plate, neither of them looking at her.

'All right.' Bryony put her hands on her hips, her eyes twinkling. 'What happened to the sprouts?'

Lizzie covered her mouth and gave a snort of laughter and Jack tried to look innocent.

'Did you know that tigers love sprouts?'

Lizzie smiled happily. 'If Jack was my daddy I'd *never* have to eat sprouts.'

Jack shot Bryony a rueful look and ran a hand over the back of his neck. 'Lizzie, angel, we've got to talk about this.'

But before he could say any more, the phone rang. Bryony picked it up, expecting it to be her mother ringing about the babysitting arrangements for that evening.

It was Toby and when she finally replaced the receiver she was silent.

'What's the matter?' Jack was feeding Lizzie the last of her fish fingers. 'Is he going to be late?'

'He isn't coming.' Bryony looked at him, thinking that Jack didn't look that surprised. He just carried on feeding Lizzie. She frowned. 'She can feed herself, Jack.'

'I know she can, but we're playing zoos,' he said

calmly, 'and at the moment I'm feeding the tigers. So why is your date off?'

'Because Sean sent him over to Penrith to pick up some equipment for the team and it's taken him ages to sort it out and he's still there.' She frowned. 'Why didn't he tell Sean that he had a date?'

Jack stabbed the last of the fish fingers, not looking at her. 'Well, I suppose it was important.'

'It sounded pretty routine to me,' Bryony muttered, facing the fact that yet another date had turned into a disaster, this time before the guy had even turned up on her doorstep. She was jinxed. Or was she?

Suddenly she looked at Jack suspiciously, remembering his attitude to Toby when they'd gone on the rescue. Had he somehow engineered this so that they couldn't go out? She knew he wasn't comfortable with the idea of her finding a daddy for Lizzie. And if she found someone, obviously that would affect his relationship because he couldn't just come and go the way he did at the moment.

Was he the reason Toby hadn't turned up?

She glanced down at herself with a sigh. 'All dressed up and nowhere to go,' she said lightly, giving a shrug. 'I suppose I may as well go and get changed.'

'Why?'

Jack stood up and suddenly all she was breathlessly aware of were those sexy blue eyes watching her.

'Well, there's no point in wearing *this*—' she gestured down to herself '—to eat baked beans.'

'Who said anything about baked beans?' he drawled softly, walking towards her with a distinct air of purpose. 'Ring your mum and cancel.'

'Cancel?'

He was so close now she could hardly breathe, and he gave her that smile that always made her insides tumble.

'Yes, cancel.' He put a hand under her chin and lifted her face to his. 'I'll cook dinner and you can wear the dress. You don't need a babysitter.'

Her heart was pumping in her chest and her whole body throbbed with a sexual awareness that was totally unfamiliar. 'You hate this dress.'

'I never said I hated the dress.'

Their eyes locked and suddenly all she could think about was that kiss. The way it had felt when his mouth had claimed hers.

She wanted him to kiss her again.

'You two are looking all funny.' Lizzie was staring at them curiously. 'Are you going to kiss?'

Bryony gasped and pulled away from Jack, her face flaming. She'd forgotten that Lizzie was still sitting at the table. 'No!' She was suddenly flustered. 'We're not going to kiss.'

'I don't mind if you do,' Lizzie said generously, sliding off her chair and carrying her plate to the dishwasher. 'Sally says it's yucky when her parents do it, but I think it would be nice.'

'Lizzie, we're not going to kiss,' Bryony muttered, not daring to look at Jack but feeling his gaze on her. She always knew when he was looking at her and he was looking at her now.

'You blush easily, Blondie, do you know that?' His voice was a soft, teasing drawl and Lizzie clapped her hands.

'Mummy only ever goes that colour when you're here, Jack.'

Deciding that the conversation had gone far enough, Bryony glanced at her watch. 'And you should be getting ready for bed, Lizzie,' she said quickly. 'Do you want Jack to read you a story?'

'Only if he doesn't skip bits.'

Bryony risked a look at Jack. 'Is that OK with you, or do you need to get going?'

'That depends…'

'On what?'

He winked at her. 'What you're cooking me for dinner—'

She rolled her eyes. 'Don't you ever go home and cook for yourself, Jack?'

'Why would I want to when I've got you to cook for me?' He smiled and held up a hand. 'Only joking. As it happens, I'm cooking for you tonight.'

'You're cooking for *me*?'

Jack never cooked. He lounged at her table, watching while she cooked. And actually she liked it that way. She found cooking relaxing and there was nothing she enjoyed more than an evening chatting with Jack.

'I'm cooking for you. A gourmet creation right under your very nose. It's your turn to be impressed, Blondie.'

'But I was going out. How can you have the ingredients for a gourmet creation?'

He stooped to pick up Lizzie. 'I just picked up a few things on my way home, in case I was hungry later.'

'But you don't even know where the supermarket

is.' Her eyes teased him. 'Or are you telling me you finally *asked for directions*?'

'No need.' He displayed his muscles, flexing his shoulders and his biceps. 'Man is a natural hunter.'

She lifted an eyebrow. 'You went to the supermarket in your *loin cloth*?'

'Of course. But I left my spear outside.' His eyes gleamed wickedly and she felt herself blush.

It was only as he walked out of the room with Lizzie that she realised that he hadn't actually answered her question about the food. How did he come to have the ingredients for a gourmet meal in his boot?

And why did he want her to keep the dress on when the last time she'd worn it he'd covered her up?

But the last time she'd worn it she'd been going out with another man.

Bryony plopped down on the nearest kitchen chair and wondered if Jack realised that he was displaying all the signs of a jealous male.

Probably not.

She hadn't realised it herself until two seconds ago.

But to be jealous you had to care, and Jack didn't care about her. Not like that.

Or did he?

She sat in silence, her mind running over everything that had happened since the night she'd walked into the pub and announced that she was going to start dating men again.

Jack had sabotaged every date.

Had he done that because of Lizzie? Because he didn't want Lizzie to have a daddy?

Or had he done it because he hadn't been able to see her with another man?

CHAPTER EIGHT

THE week before Christmas Jack, Bryony and Sean were in the staffroom discussing the mountain rescue team Christmas party, when Nicky rushed in, looking stressed.

'I just had a call from Ambulance Control,' she said breathlessly. 'Ellie has driven her car into a ditch.'

'Our Ellie?' Jack was on his feet immediately, his expression concerned. 'She's nearly eight months pregnant. Is she OK?'

Nicky shook her head. 'I haven't got many details but they had to cut her out of the car.'

Bryony was already hurrying to the door.

'She's been poorly right the way through this pregnancy,' Sean muttered, and Bryony remembered that he was very friendly with the couple outside work. 'That's why she gave up work early. Has anyone called Ben? This is his wife we're talking about.'

Ben MacAllister was another of the A and E consultants, and Ellie had worked as a nurse in A and E before she'd become pregnant.

'He's away on that immediate care course,' Jack reminded him, and Sean swore softly.

'Well, someone get on the phone.'

They heard the ambulance siren and Jack turned to Bryony. 'Call Tom,' he said urgently. 'I don't know

146

whether there's a problem with the baby, but we're not taking any chances and I want your brother here.'

Without questioning his decision, Bryony hurried to the phone and called her brother and then hurried to Resus where the paramedics had taken Ellie.

Jack and Sean were already examining her thoroughly.

'Is Tom coming?' Jack was giving Ellie oxygen, clearly concerned about the baby.

'He's in Theatre, doing an emergency section,' Bryony told him, trying to hide her shock at seeing Ellie on the trolley. Her face was paper white and her blonde hair was matted with blood. 'He'll be down as soon as he can.'

Jack nodded and touched Ellie on the shoulder, lifting the mask away from her face for a moment. 'You're going to be fine, Ellie,' he said softly. 'The scalp wound is quite superficial. How are you feeling?'

'Worried about the baby,' Ellie said weakly, her normal exuberance extinguished by the shock of the accident and the pain she was in. 'Has someone called Ben?'

'He's on his way,' Nicky told her quickly, and Ellie gave a groan and closed her eyes.

'He'll be so worried—I wasn't sure whether we should have called him really...'

'He'd want to know,' Sean said, his face unusually white and strained as he looked at his friend lying on the trolley. 'What the hell were you doing, driving your car into a ditch anyway?'

Bryony saw Ellie smile and she lifted the oxygen mask from her face so that she could answer.

'I swerved to avoid a sheep,' she croaked, and Sean rolled his eyes.

'Well, of course you did,' he said gruffly, and looked at Jack. 'This is your show.'

Jack nodded and Bryony knew that Sean was handing over responsibility to someone who wasn't so close to Ellie. He was obviously finding it hard to be objective.

'Nicky, I need a pad for that scalp wound. We can glue it later.' Jack smiled down at Ellie. 'You're going to be fine, but I'm going to put a couple of lines in and check the baby.'

His voice was smooth and confident and he held out a hand to Nicky who'd already anticipated everything they were going to need.

Ellie shifted slightly on the trolley. 'I'm bleeding, Jack,' she murmured, her eyes drifting shut. 'I can feel it. Oh, God, I can't believe this is happening again. I'm going to lose it, I know I'm going to lose it.'

'You're not going to lose this baby,' Jack said firmly, his swift glance towards Bryony communicating clearly that she should call her brother again.

Bryony called Theatre again, and explained the situation. In the meantime Sean had put two lines in, and Ellie was connected to various monitors and had an IV running.

'Blondie, I want BMG, coagulation screen, rhesus/antibody status and a Kleihauer test. The foetal heart rate is good,' Jack said softly, his eyes on the monitor. 'Ellie, I'm just going to feel your uterus—I want you to keep that oxygen mask on now, please. No more talking, sweetheart.'

But Ellie clutched his arm. 'If Tom can't get here, I want you to section me,' she croaked, her eyes suddenly swimming with tears. 'Don't let me lose this baby, Jack. Please, don't let me lose this baby.'

Jack's eyes locked on hers, his gaze wonderfully confident and reassuring. 'If I have to section you here, I can and I will,' he promised, 'and you are not going to lose this baby, Ellie. I swear it. Trust me, angel.' He looked at Nicky. 'Get me a pack ready just in case. And someone tell Tom Hunter that if he doesn't get himself down here in the next two minutes, he's buying the drinks for the whole of next year.'

Swallowing back a lump in her throat, Bryony took blood and arranged for it to be sent to the lab, someone delivered the portable ultrasound machine and Jack carefully scanned Ellie's abdomen, staring at the screen with total concentration as he looked for problems. He squinted closer at one area and exchanged glances with Sean who gave a discreet nod.

'The foetal heart is still 140,' Jack said, carrying on with the ultrasound until he was satisfied with what he'd seen.

Ellie tried to move the mask and Jack put a hand on hers to prevent her, anticipating her question.

'The baby is fine,' he said softly. 'I can see the heart beating and he just kicked me really hard. He's better in than out at the moment.'

Ellie gave a weak smile and closed her eyes again just as Tom strode into the room.

'Sorry, folks—tricky section upstairs. How are you doing here?'

Jack briefed him quickly and Tom listened carefully, asking the occasional question, his eyes flickering to Ellie who had her eyes closed. For once he and Jack were serious, no trace of their usual banter or humour as they conferred. Tom washed his hands and approached the trolley.

'Hi, Ellie,' he said gently, 'it's Tom. I just want to check on that baby of yours.'

Ellie's eyes opened and she looked frightened as she pulled the mask away from her face. 'I want you to deliver it, Tom,' she croaked. 'Deliver it now. Please. I've got one of my feelings. A very bad feeling...'

Tom squeezed her shoulder briefly and then slid the blanket down so that he could look at her abdomen. 'Trust me, Ellie,' he said gently. 'I'm not going to let you lose this baby.'

'I marked the top of the fundus,' Jack told him and Tom nodded as he examined Ellie thoroughly.

Five minutes later he glanced at Jack. 'She's bleeding quite a bit. I'm going to section her. Is there anything I need to know? Has she had a head injury?'

'She has a minor scalp laceration but she wasn't knocked out and her cervical spine is fine,' Jack told him. 'She's all yours.'

Tom ran a hand over the back of his neck. 'Is Ben coming?'

Ellie looked at him, her face pale. 'Just do it, Tom,' she whispered. 'Don't wait for Ben. Sean, will you stay with me?'

Sean stepped forward. 'Try getting rid of me,' he said gruffly, taking Ellie's hand in his. 'Let's get her up to the labour ward and get this baby out.'

Everything happened swiftly after that.

Sean and Jack transferred Ellie up to the labour ward while Tom phoned around and called in the assistance of the top anaesthetist and two paediatricians, and then he sprinted up to Theatre after them.

Bryony and Nicky cleared up Resus, both of them quiet and worried about Ellie. They were still talking quietly, enjoying a brief lull in the usual run of patients, when Ben strode into Resus, his face drawn with worry.

'Where is she?'

'In Theatre on the labour ward,' Bryony said immediately. 'Tom is sectioning her.'

Ben sprinted back out of the room and Nicky sighed.

'There goes a man in love. I remember when those two met. Ellie just wouldn't let the man say no. Now he can barely let her out of his sight.'

'Ellie will be fine,' Bryony said firmly. 'Tom is a brilliant obstetrician.'

She had every faith in her brother, and every faith in Jack. Surely there was no way that anything could happen to Ellie or her baby?

'To baby MacAllister, as yet unnamed, and to Jack and Tom—' Sean raised his glass '—and a job well done.'

The whole mountain rescue team was gathered in the Drunken Fox to celebrate the safe arrival of Ben and Ellie's little boy.

Despite being just over four weeks early, he was doing well and was with Ellie on the ward.

Tom slung an arm round Jack's shoulders, his expression solemn. 'Just a question of knowing how, wouldn't you agree?'

'Absolutely.' Jack nodded sagely. 'That and natural brilliance.'

Tom reached for his beer. 'And years of training.'

'And finely honed instincts.'

Bryony rolled her eyes. 'And massive egos.' She looked at Sean. 'Better book two extra places at the Christmas party just to make room.'

There was general laughter and the conversation switched to the annual Christmas bash.

Bryony slid onto a barstool. 'So it's tomorrow night?'

'The venue has changed,' Sean told everyone, and Bryony frowned when she heard where it was.

'But that's miles away.'

'Over the other side of the valley,' Sean agreed, 'and if the weather carries on like this we'll have to all go in the four-wheel-drives or we'll be stuck in snowdrifts.'

'That would make a good newspaper headline,' Tom said mildly. 'ENTIRE MOUNTAIN RESCUE TEAM RESCUED FROM SNOWDRIFT.'

'It would be too embarrassing for words,' Jack agreed with a mock shudder, 'and it isn't going to happen.'

'Think of his ego,' Bryony said seriously, her blue eyes wide. 'It might never recover from the shock of such a public humiliation. It might shrivel to nothing.'

Sean finished his drink. 'We'll meet at the rescue centre at seven and go from there.'

'Bryony and I don't finish work until seven.' Jack

reached for his jacket. 'I'll drive her there in the Ferrari.'

Sean gaped at him. 'You're taking your Ferrari out on these roads? You'll land it in a ditch.'

'I will not.' Jack looked affronted. 'I am invincible.'

'And so modest,' Bryony said mildly.

In the end they were late leaving A and E and Bryony struggled into her dress in the staff toilet, thinking longingly of scented bubble baths and hairdressers. Most people spent hours getting ready for a Christmas party. She had less than five minutes and she could already hear Jack leaning on the horn of the Ferrari.

'All right, all right, I'm here.' She fell into the seat next to him, her work clothes stuffed haphazardly into a bag, her blonde hair tumbling over her shoulders. 'I haven't even had a chance to do my hair.'

'You can do it on the way. We're already late.' Jack reversed the car out of his space and drove off in the direction of the next valley.

Bryony rummaged in her bag for her hairclips and gave a groan of frustration. 'I think I left them at work.'

'Left what at work?'

'My new hair slide.'

Jack glanced towards her and frowned. 'You look great. Leave it down.'

Bryony lifted a hand and touched her hair self-consciously. 'I look as though I've just woken up.'

'Precisely.' Jack gave her a wicked smile, his voice a lazy, masculine drawl. 'As I said—you look great.'

Was he flirting with her?

Bryony felt her stomach turn over and she looked at him, trying to read his mind, but he was concentrating on the road again. She stared at his strong profile, her gaze lingering on his mouth.

Something felt different about their relationship, but she wasn't sure what. He hadn't laid a finger on her since that one incredible kiss, but something was different. He looked at her differently.

'I can't think why Sean booked it all the way out here,' Jack grumbled as he turned the car up a narrow road and put his foot down. 'There must have been somewhere closer.'

'He wanted to just give us a grid reference and see where we all ended up,' Bryony told him, removing her gaze from his mouth with a huge effort. 'At least we managed to talk him out of that one. Do you want me to look at a map?'

'I know where I'm going.'

Bryony looked at him in surprise. 'You've been here before?'

'No.' Jack glanced across and gave her a sexy wink. 'But men have an instinctive sense of direction.'

Bryony rolled her eyes. 'Which means we're about to get lost.'

But they didn't get lost and less than twenty minutes later Jack pulled into the restaurant car park with a smug smile.

'I am invincible.'

'Unbearable, more like,' Bryony muttered, shivering as she opened the door and the cold hit her. 'It's going to snow again. It's freezing.'

'Men don't notice the cold.' Jack locked the car

and held out a hand. 'Don't want you to slip, Blondie.'

'Believe it or not, I can put one foot in front of the other quite effectively,' she said tartly. 'I've been practising hard lately and I've finally got the hang of it.'

Ignoring his outstretched hand, she stalked towards the restaurant with as much dignity as she could given the amount of ice and snow on the path. She didn't dare take his hand. She was afraid she might never want to let go.

The rest of the team was already there and they had a fantastic evening, laughing and eating and drinking. Halfway through Jack looked at Bryony.

'You seem to be on water. How do you fancy driving the Ferrari home tonight?'

Her eyes gleamed. 'You trust me to drive your Ferrari on ice?'

'I'll be beside you. What can go wrong?'

But when they finally left the restaurant, several inches of snow had fallen and Bryony looked at the road doubtfully.

'I'm not sure about driving—we could cadge a lift in one of the four-wheel-drives.'

'They're full,' Jack told her, pushing her gently towards the car. 'You'll be fine.'

Bryony drove slowly but gradually she got the feel of the car and her confidence increased. Surprised by the lack of teasing from the passenger seat, she glanced sideways at Jack and realised that he'd fallen asleep.

Turning her attention back to the road, she turned

right and followed the road for a while then gradually realised that it didn't look at all familiar.

She carried on for a while, hoping to see a sign of some sort, but there was nothing. The snow was falling heavily now and she could barely see the road in front of her so it was a relief when she saw the lights of a pub ahead. At least they'd be able to find out where they were.

She stopped the car and Jack gave a yawn.

'Are we home?'

Bryony slumped back in her seat and braced herself for some serious teasing. 'I haven't got a clue where we are.'

There was a moment's silence while Jack squinted at the pub. 'Well, if you had to get us lost, Blondie, at least you did it by a pub,' he said mildly, undoing his seat belt and opening the car door.

'Where are you going?' She stared at him. 'Are you asking for directions?'

He grinned. 'Of course I'm not asking for directions. I'm a man. But I'm going to check whether the road is open further on. My ego doesn't want to spend the night stuck in a snowdrift. It isn't well enough insulated.'

He vanished into the pub and reappeared moments later, his expression serious. 'As I thought, the road is blocked ahead and they won't be able to clear it until the morning. We can stay here for the night. Do you need to ring your mum?'

Bryony shook her head and unfastened her seat belt. 'She's got Lizzie until tomorrow night. They're going Christmas shopping together tomorrow.'

'Great. In which case, we'll stay here for the night

and they can clear the road while someone cooks me bacon, sausages and mushrooms for breakfast,' Jack said cheerfully, holding the door open and grabbing her arm so that she didn't slip.

'I haven't got anything to sleep in,' Bryony protested, and Jack shrugged, pushing open the door of the pub and hustling her into the warmth.

'You can sleep in your underwear,' he drawled, 'unless you'd rather sleep in mine.'

She shot him a withering look and the amusement in his blue eyes deepened.

'Just a suggestion.'

The landlady smiled at Jack and handed over a key. 'It's the last room. You're lucky. It's the honeymoon suite. We did it up specially because we have so many couples up here looking for somewhere to spend a romantic night.'

Bryony followed Jack up a flight of stairs, a frown on her face. 'The last room? There's only one room? And it's the honeymoon suite?'

'It'll be fine.' He unlocked the door. 'I'll sleep in the armchair.'

But there wasn't an armchair. Just an enormous bed draped in fur and satin, a small dressing room and a huge, marble bathroom.

They looked at each other and Bryony gave a snort of laughter as she saw Jack's face.

'It's the honeymoon suite, Jack,' she cooed, unable to resist teasing him and he shook his head, gazing round the room in disbelief.

'I knew there was a reason I never wanted to get married.' He peered at the bed in amazement. 'Hasn't Lizzie got a bed just like that for one of her dolls?'

'There's no chair,' Bryony said, glancing round for some alternative suggestion. 'You'll just have to sleep on the floor.'

'There's no way I'm sleeping on a fluffy carpet.' Jack ripped off his jacket and dropped it over the end of the bed. 'That's an emperor-size bed at least. There's plenty of room for two of us in that. And if we shut our eyes tightly we can probably forget about the satin and fur.'

Bryony stared at him. He was suggesting that they sleep in the same bed?

Jack took one look at her face and lifted an eyebrow in question. 'We've known each other for twenty-two years, for goodness' sake. Don't you trust me, Blondie?'

Bryony looked at the bed and swallowed. She trusted him. It was herself she didn't trust. But she could hardly protest without revealing what she felt for him.

So she'd climb into the bed, turn her back on him and try and forget it was Jack lying next to her. It wasn't as if the bed was small...

Throwing a casual smile in his direction, she walked into the enormous bathroom and closed the door firmly behind her. *Oh, help!*

She stared at herself in the mirror and wondered whether she should just sleep in her dress. It was either that or take it off, and if she took it off...

She was still standing there five minutes later when Jack banged on the door. 'Have you been sucked down the plughole or something? Hurry up!'

Bryony closed her eyes briefly and then decided that she may as well get on with it. He was obviously totally indifferent to the fact that they were about to spend a night in the same bed, so perhaps she could be, too.

She used the toiletries and then opened the bathroom door and gave him a bright smile.

'All yours. You're going to *love* the mermaid taps.'

She strolled past him, waited until she heard the door close and then wriggled out of her dress and leaped into the bed, still wearing her underwear. The bed was huge and absolutely freezing and she lay there, her whole body shivering, wondering how she was ever going to sleep.

She heard sounds of the shower running and then finally the door opened and Jack appeared, a towel wrapped around his hips.

Bryony's heart started to thud rhythmically in her chest and suddenly she didn't feel cold any more.

She'd seen his body before, of course. In the summer at the beach. In the swimming pool when they'd taken Lizzie together. But she'd never seen his body when she was lying half-naked in bed. Suddenly all she could think about was the fact that he was about to slide in between the sheets next to her.

And he wasn't wearing anything.

In the dim light of the bedroom he was breathtakingly sexy. Her eyes followed the line of his body hair, tracking down over his muscular chest, down his board-flat stomach and down further still until it disappeared under the towel.

Refusing to allow herself to even think about what was underneath the towel, Bryony forced herself to breathe before she passed out. 'Are you planning to wear a towel to bed?' she croaked, trying to keep it light but feeling anything but light. In fact, her whole body felt heavy.

Jack eyed the bed with amusement. 'This bed is huge. I'm going to need a grid reference to find you.'

'You don't have to find me,' Bryony said hastily. 'It's really late. Just go to sleep.'

And with that she rolled over and closed her eyes tightly. Not that it made any difference at all. Even with her eyes shut she could still see every inch of his incredible body. The image was embedded in her brain and when she felt the bed dip slightly and heard him switch the light off, she curled her fingers into the duvet to stop herself from reaching for him.

For a moment neither of them moved and then he cursed softly. 'I'm developing frostbite. This bed is freezing.'

'Just go to sleep, Jack.'

'I can't go to sleep, my teeth are chattering too much.'

She gave a sigh and turned towards him, telling herself that it was dark anyway so she couldn't see him and he couldn't see her.

'Well, go and put your shirt back on.'

'I'm not sleeping in my clothes.'

She chuckled. 'Put my clothes on, then.'

'Good idea. I could wear your dress as a T-shirt.' He gave a shiver. 'Alternatively, we could cuddle each other. Warm me up, woman, or I'll be found dead in the morning.'

Before she could anticipate his next move, he reached for her and pulled her firmly against him so that they were lying side by side and nose to nose.

'Jack!' She tensed and planted her hands firmly on

the centre of his chest and pushed against him, but he didn't budge.

'Just relax, will you?' His voice sounded very male in the darkness. 'You know as well as I do that bodily warmth is an important source of heat.'

A source of heat?

Being this close to him, her fingers tangled with the hairs on his chest, her palms feeling the steady thud of his heart. It wasn't heat she was producing, it was fire.

And she realised that he wasn't cold at all. His body was warm and hard and throbbing with vital masculinity and it was pressed against hers.

'Jack, I can't—'

'Shut up, Blondie.' He slid a hand round the back of her neck and found her mouth with his. His tongue traced the seam of her lips and her mouth opened under his, breathing in his groan of desire.

'Jack, this is a mistake.'

'Probably.' His mouth was warm against hers, his kiss maddeningly seductive. 'But I like making mistakes. It's the only thing that prevents me from being completely perfect.'

She chortled and thumped his shoulder. Or at least she meant to thump his shoulder, but somehow her fist uncurled itself and she slid a shaking hand over the smooth skin, feeling the powerful swell of muscle under her fingers.

'Jack…' This time her voice was a whisper and he rolled her onto her back and covered her body with his.

'Stop talking.' He brought his mouth down on hers and kissed her again and suddenly she was kissing him back. And it felt like all her dreams because darkness was where she always dreamed about Jack, and when she dreamed, this was always what he was doing.

Kissing her.

And in the darkness the rest of the world ceased to exist. There was only Jack and the seductive brush of his mouth against hers, the erotic slide of his tongue and the weight of his body holding her still.

She felt his hand slide down her body and then his fingers found her tight, aching nipple through the silky fabric of her bra. She arched into his hand and he deepened the kiss, seducing her with every stroke of his tongue and every brush of his fingers. He removed her bra with an expert flick of his fingers and then reached out and switched on the lamp by the bed.

Bryony gave a gasp and looked at him in confusion. 'What are you doing?'

'Looking at you.' The expression in his eyes was disturbingly intense. 'I'm looking at you.'

Colour seeped into her cheeks and she reached out a hand to switch off the light, but he caught her arm and pinned it above her head.

'Jack, please…'

'I want to look at you because you're beautiful, Blondie, do you know that?' His voice was hoarse and he dragged the covers back, his eyes sliding down her body with male appreciation. Then he lifted a hand and touched her hair, running his fingers through it and stroking it as if he was seeing it for the first time.

She lay beneath him, powerless to move, watching

in breathless anticipation as hunger flared in his eyes. It was the look she'd always dreamed of seeing and suddenly her breathing was shallow and every nerve ending in her body tingled.

She didn't know what had finally changed for him but she wasn't going to question it.

For a suspended moment they stared at each other, and then he brought his mouth down hard on hers.

Her hunger was every bit as intense as his and she kissed him back, sliding her arms around his neck, her heart beating frantically as she arched against him. He kissed her until she was crazy for something more and then he lifted his head fractionally, his breathing unsteady as he looked down at her. His eyes glittered strangely in the dim light and for once there was no trace of humour in his expression.

'Do you want me to stop?' His voice was husky with unfulfilled desire and her own breathing jerked in response to this blatant evidence of masculine arousal.

'No.' Her hand slid down the warm, smooth skin of his back. 'Don't stop.'

Something flared in his eyes and he slid down her body, his tongue finding a path down her sensitised skin. His mouth closed over the tip of one breast and she cried out, sensation stabbing the very heart of her. He teased her skilfully with slow flicks of his clever tongue and then, when she was writhing and sobbing beneath him, he sucked her into the heat of his mouth and she gasped and sank her fingers into his dark hair, holding him against her. She shifted restlessly, trying to relieve the throbbing ache between her thighs.

Immediately his hand slid downwards, ready to satisfy her unspoken request.

With a swift movement he removed her panties and then moved back up her body until he was staring down at her, his glittering blue eyes holding her captive as his hand rested on her most intimate place. He looked dark and dangerous and unbelievably sexy and she was burning with a sexual excitement so intense that she felt as though her whole body was on fire.

And then he bent his head and took her mouth in a slow, seductive kiss and she gasped as she felt his long fingers stroking her for the first time. He explored her with an expert touch, the maddening caress of his fingers driving her wild. And all the time his eyes held hers, stripping down all the barriers between them, his gaze every bit as intimate as his touch.

She lifted a hand and ran her fingers over his rough jaw, loving the male contrast to her own softness. And suddenly she wanted to touch him as he was touching her. Her hand trailed over his wide shoulders and down his powerful body until her fingers closed around the pulsing heat of his arousal. He felt hot and hard and excitingly male and she stroked him gently until he muttered something under his breath and reached down.

'Stop.' His voice was thickened as his hand closed over her wrist. 'You need to give me a minute.'

But she didn't want to give him a minute. She was *desperate*, her body driven to fever pitch by his skilled touch.

She curled her legs around him, consumed by a feminine need so powerful that she raked his back with her nails in desperation.

'Jack, *please…*'

Breathing heavily, he slid an arm beneath her and she felt the silken probe of his erection against her. She arched invitingly and he entered her with a hard, demanding thrust, filling her with a heat and passion that she'd only known in her dreams.

She cried out in ecstasy and he gave a groan and thrust deeper still, his eyes locking with hers, fierce with passion. And she was lost in that gaze, the connection between them so powerful that she felt part of him.

'*Bryony—*'

It was the first time she could ever remember him calling her by her name and she stared into his eyes, overwhelmed by emotion and sensation, every part of her body feeling every part of his. And then he started to move slowly and with every measured thrust he seemed to move deeper inside her, closer to her heart. She felt his strength and his power and was consumed by a rush of pleasure so agonisingly intense that she sobbed against the sleek muscle of his shoulder. She clung to him, fevered and breathless, totally out of control and not even caring. Every time her eyes drifted shut he muttered, 'Open your eyes.' And so she did, and finally she couldn't look away as he drove her higher and higher until finally she felt the world explode and her whole body convulse in an ecstasy so powerful that it pushed him over the edge and she felt the hot, hard pulse of his own climax.

It was so powerful that for several minutes neither of them spoke. They just held each other, breathing unsteadily, their gazes still locked, sharing a depth of emotion that neither of them had felt before.

And then finally he gave a small, disbelieving shake of his head and rolled onto his back, taking her with him.

Bryony lay against him and allowed her eyes to drift shut, so utterly swamped with happiness that she started to smile.

Jack loved her.

She'd seen it in his eyes when he'd stared down at her. And she'd felt it in the way he'd made love to her.

Jack *definitely* loved her.

CHAPTER NINE

SHE awoke feeling warm and safe, wrapped tightly in his arms.

Bryony's body ached in unfamiliar places and she smiled as she remembered every tiny detail of the night before. She snuggled closer to him and kissed him gently on the mouth, watching as he woke up.

'I love you, Jack.'

Finally she could say the words she'd been longing to say for almost all her life.

And she sensed his immediate withdrawal. Physically he didn't move, but she saw something flicker in his eyes and felt his lack of response with every fibre of her being. Her insides lurched.

'Listen, Blondie.' His voice cracked slightly and he cursed under his breath and released her, rolling onto his back and staring up at the ceiling. His eyes were shut and a tiny muscle worked in his rough jaw. 'About last night...'

'*Don't* call me Blondie,' she said, her voice shaking as she lifted herself on one elbow and looked at him. *She wasn't going to let him do this*. She wasn't going to let him pretend that what they'd shared hadn't been special. 'Do you realise that last night you called me Bryony for the first time in your life? That was when you were making love to me, Jack.'

His eyes stayed closed. 'I thought we agreed that last night was a mistake.'

'It wasn't a mistake for me.' She knew she was taking a huge risk but there was no turning back now. 'I love you, Jack.'

His eyes flew open and he stared at her for a moment. Then he sucked in a breath and sprang out of bed so quickly that she blinked in amazement.

'Blond— Sorry, *Bryony*,' he corrected himself quickly as he reached for his clothes. 'You do not love me, all right? You just *think* you love me because last night we had sex and women think soppy thoughts after sex.'

She watched, thinking that she'd never seen anyone dress so quickly in her whole life. Trousers, shirt, jumper—in seconds he was fully clothed, his expression desperate as he searched for his boots.

'Why are you panicking, Jack?'

'I'm not panicking.' He found his boots and dragged them on without untying the laces. 'I just think we need to get going.'

'You are panicking. You're panicking because I told you that I love you.'

He scowled at her and ran both hands through his already tousled dark hair. 'I'm not panicking about that, because I know it isn't true.'

'It *is* true.' She took a deep breath. 'And I know you love me, too.'

He went completely still, his eyes fixed on her as if she were a dangerous animal that could attack at any moment. Then he swore under his breath and gave a sigh.

'Bryony.' He said her name firmly. 'We spent the night together, sweetheart. We had good—' He broke off with a frown '—well, *amazing*, actually...' He cleared his throat. 'We had amazing sex. It doesn't mean we're in love.'

'Of course it doesn't.' She sat up in the bed, deriving considerable satisfaction from the way that his eyes lingered hungrily on her breasts before she tucked the duvet under her arms. 'But we were in love before we had sex. The sex was amazing *because* we're in love. You felt it, too, Jack. I know you did. I saw it in your eyes. I *felt* it, Jack.'

'What do you mean—we were in love before we had sex?' He licked dry lips and his eyes flicked towards the door. 'We've been friends for twenty-two years, Blondie. We love each other, of course we do, but not *like that*.'

'I love you *like that*,' Bryony said quietly, 'and I always have.'

There was a long, tense silence and then he shook his head. 'We both know that isn't true. There's Lizzie's father for a start.'

Bryony felt her heart thump heavily in her chest. She'd never talked about Lizzie's father to anyone before. Never.

'Lizzie's father was my one attempt to get you out of my system,' she said quietly, watching as his face drained of colour. 'I've loved you all my life, Jack, but I resigned myself to the fact that you were never going to marry anyone. I decided that I needed to stop dreaming about you and get on with my life.'

He was staring at her. 'That isn't true.'

'It's true. I met Lizzie's father at a party. He was good-looking and fun to be with—'

Jack's mouth tightened. 'Spare me the details.'

'I thought you wanted the details.'

'I *don't* want to know that you found him attractive,' he grated, and Bryony stared at him in exasperation, wondering if he realised just how contradictory he was being. One minute he was saying that he didn't love her and the next he was showing all the signs of extreme jealousy.

'We spent the night together,' she said finally. 'I was determined to forget about you.'

'And it worked, yes?' His eyes glittered strangely. 'I mean, you've never given even the slightest hint that you cared about me, so it must have worked.'

She sighed. 'I didn't give the slightest hint that I cared about you because you would have done what you're doing now. Panic. And, no, it didn't work. At least, not in the sense that you mean. It taught me that I'm a one-man woman, and that man is you, Jack.'

'But you slept with him.'

She blushed and gave a wry smile. 'Just the once.'

'And then you slept with other men—yes?'

She shook her head. 'No other men. There didn't seem any point when none of them were you.'

He ran a hand over the back of his neck, visibly shaken by her admission. 'You're saying that last night was only the second time you've had sex in your life?'

She nodded. 'That's right, Jack. Why? Did I disappoint?'

There was a faint sheen of sweat on his brow. 'You know you didn't disappoint.' He let out a long breath and closed his eyes briefly. 'Blond—Bryony, I don't know what to say.'

'Say that you love me, too,' she croaked, 'because I know you do, Jack. I saw it in your eyes last night.'

He shook his head, his expression bleak as he looked at her. 'I can't say that.' His voice was hoarse. 'I wish I could, but I can't. You know I don't do commitment, Bryony.'

'Yes, you do.' She tipped her head on one side and watched him. 'You have been there for me for every second of the last twenty-two years, Jack, and since Lizzie was born you've been there for her, too. If that isn't commitment, then I don't know what is. I *know* you love me, Jack.'

She knew she was pushing him and her heart was thudding in her chest as she anticipated his reaction. Maybe it was the wrong thing to do, but what did she have to lose?

He shook his head. 'I can't be what you want me to be. I'd let you down. I'd let Lizzie down.'

'I don't believe that,' she said softly. 'I know that you had a terrible childhood. I know that your parents had a terrible marriage, but they never loved each other. That was so obvious. We do. We *really* love each other. We were always meant to be together.'

'Is that why you slept with me last night?' His eyes burned into hers. 'Because you thought I'd say—I'd say those three words?'

Which he couldn't even bring himself to say as part of a conversation, Bryony observed sadly.

'I slept with you because it felt right and because I love you,' she said quietly. 'I'm not trying to trap you, Jack. You're my best friend. It's just that I know you love me, too.'

'That's not true.'

'Jack.' Her tone was patient. 'Since November I've been dating other men. Or, at least, I've been trying to. It hasn't been going that well and lately I've been asking myself why.'

He looked at her warily. 'And what has that got to do with me?'

'Everything.' She stared at him and sighed. 'Jack, that first night I went out with David. You hated my dress. You said it was indecent.'

'It was indecent.'

'But the other night you wanted me to wear it for you. You didn't find it indecent then.'

Hot colour touched his cheekbones and he breathed in sharply. 'That's different.'

'You wouldn't let me invite him in for coffee, you wouldn't let him drive me home…' She listed the various incidents and he grew steadily more tense.

'I never said I didn't care about you,' he said stiffly, 'but just because I don't want you to marry the wrong man doesn't mean I love you. You're reading too much into it, which is a typically female pastime.'

'Is it?' She looked at him calmly. 'Where do you spend most of your free time, Jack? Do you go home?'

'I have an active social life.'

'Which basically means that you have sex with different women,' she said gently, 'but you don't spend time with those women, do you, Jack? You have a massive house but you never go there. You spend time with me. In *my* house. Sitting in my kitchen. Chatting about everything. Being part of my life. And Lizzie's life.'

'You're my friend.'

She nodded. 'And that's the best thing about a good marriage. I know because I saw it in my parents' marriage. In a good marriage you are friends as well as lovers.'

He backed away and stared at her incredulously. 'You're proposing to me?'

'No.' She held her breath. 'I'm waiting for you to propose to me, Jack. And then we can spend the rest of our lives having fantastic sex and enjoying the special friendship we've always had. And Lizzie gets the daddy she's always dreamed of.'

He stared at her for a suspended moment and then he grabbed his jacket. 'No.' He thrust his arms into the jacket and zipped it up firmly, his jaw set in a hard line. 'I think you've gone mad. For me it was just sex, Blondie—great sex, but just sex.'

'Jack—'

His eyes blazed into hers. 'We won't talk about it again.'

'*Jack!*'

'I'll go and warm the engine up.'

'Why are men like mascara?' Bryony murmured to herself, watching him go with tears in her eyes. 'Because they run at the first sign of emotion.'

'I bet Lizzie is excited about Christmas.' Nicky handed Bryony a syringe and she slowly injected the antibiotic into the patient's vein.

'Of course.' Bryony didn't look at her. 'It's Christmas Eve tomorrow.'

'What have you bought her?'

'Oh, you know, all the usual girly things. Stuff for

her hair, lots of stuff for her dolls, a new doll that she likes.'

Everything under the sun except the one thing she wanted.

A daddy.

And she still hadn't confessed to Lizzie that Santa wasn't going to manage to deliver her the present she wanted this year.

'Are you all right?' As they moved away from the patient, Nicky touched her arm. 'You're so quiet and you look really pale.'

'I'm fine, really.' Bryony gave her a wan smile. 'Just tired and looking forward to the Christmas break.'

Nicky was frowning. 'Well, you've certainly been working long hours for the past few days, thanks to Jack doing a vanishing act. Do you know where he's gone?'

Bryony shook her head. After their night in the honeymoon suite, he'd driven her home in brooding silence, dropped her off without saying a word and then disappeared from her life. Even Sean didn't know where he was, although he did confess that Jack had called him and told him that he needed time off.

Bryony sighed. So not only had she frightened Jack off a relationship, she'd frightened him out of her life altogether.

She'd thrown herself into her work and had seen a steady stream of fractures and bruises as people had slipped on the ice, and she'd dealt with quite a few road accidents as people stupidly decided to drive home after Christmas parties.

And that night when she tucked Lizzie in she felt a huge lump in her throat.

'Lizzie…' She settled herself on the edge of the bed and took a deep breath. 'We need to talk, sweetheart.'

'Mmm?' Lizzie snuggled down, her beautiful round cheeks pink from excitement.

Bryony couldn't bear the thought that she was about to dim that excitement, but she knew that she had to say something. She couldn't let Lizzie carry on believing that Santa was going to deliver a daddy for Christmas.

'Sweetheart, you remember your letter to Santa?'

Lizzie nodded. 'I wrote it ages ago.'

'I know you did.' Bryony swallowed. 'But you also said you did it in November because you wanted to give Santa time, because you knew it was a pretty hard present for him to find.'

'That's right.' Lizzie smiled. 'And he's had *ages*.'

'It isn't a time thing, Lizzie,' Bryony said softly, reached out and brushing her daughter's face with her finger. 'And a daddy isn't really something that Santa can bring you.' Tears spilled down her cheeks and she scrubbed them away quickly, not wanting her daughter to see her cry. 'It's up to me to find you a daddy, and so far I haven't managed it.' She broke off, totally choked by emotion and afraid to say anything else in case she started to sob.

Lizzie sat up and curled her little arms round her neck. 'Don't be sad. You don't have to find a daddy for me. That's why I asked Santa. So that you don't have to worry about it.'

Bryony shook her head, tears clogging her lashes. 'Lizzie, no, he can't—'

'I've been good,' Lizzie said firmly, climbing onto Bryony's lap. 'I've been so good sometimes I've almost burst. And once I've got my daddy I'm never speaking to Sally again because she's just *horrid*.'

Bryony smiled through her tears and stroked her daughter's hair. 'I know you've been good, angel, but it doesn't make any difference. Santa can't get you a daddy. I should have told you that before. He can get you toys and things like that, but not a daddy.'

'Just wait and see.' Lizzie gave her a smug smile and nestled down in her bed. 'Night-night.'

Bryony closed her eyes. 'Night-night.'

What was she supposed to do? She'd just have to wait until Christmas morning and hope that all the other presents that she'd chosen would compensate in some small way for not being able to produce a daddy.

But she knew that her daughter was heading for a crushing disappointment.

Bryony worked the morning of Christmas Eve and there was still no sign of Jack.

'I think he's at home,' Sean said when she tentatively asked if he knew where Jack was.

Bryony frowned, knowing that it was very unlikely that Jack would be at home. He hardly spent any time at home, especially not at Christmas. He either stayed at her house or camped out with Tom or Oliver or stayed in his room at the hospital.

'Are you spending Christmas with your mother?'

Sean pulled on his coat and reached for his mobile phone.

'Lizzie and I are staying in our house tonight,' Bryony told him, 'and then we're all going to Mum's for lunch tomorrow. Tom and Oliver will be there, too, patients permitting.'

Sean lifted an eyebrow. 'And Jack?'

She shrugged. 'I don't know. He usually comes but this year…' She broke off and flashed a smile at Sean, suddenly needing to get away. 'Are you off to see Ellie and the baby?'

Sean nodded. 'They're being discharged this afternoon, all being well.'

'Give her my love.'

They went in different directions and Bryony drove to her mother's, picked up Lizzie and headed for home.

Lizzie was so excited she was bouncing in her seat like a kangaroo and Bryony felt something tug at her heart.

'It would be great if Santa brought you that nice new doll you saw,' she said, but Lizzie shook her head.

'I don't want to be greedy. A daddy is enough.'

And after that Bryony fell silent, totally unable to find a way of persuading her daughter that her dream might not come true.

She cooked tea with a cheerful smile, hung the stocking on the end of Lizzie's bed and left a mince pie and a glass of whisky by the fire for Santa.

'Do you think he'd like more than one mince pie?' Lizzie asked, and Bryony shook her head.

'He's going to eat a mince pie in every house. That's rather a lot, don't you think?'

'Can we leave carrots for the reindeer?'

'Sure.' Bryony smiled and fished in the vegetable basket, hoping that Santa's reindeer weren't too fussy. Her carrots had definitely seen better days.

Lizzie bounced and fussed and squashed some of her other presents but finally she was bathed and in her pyjamas.

'This is going to be the best Christmas ever.' She hugged Bryony and snuggled down, her eyes squeezed tightly shut. 'Santa won't come while I'm awake so I'm going straight to sleep.'

Bryony bit her lip and then bent to kiss her daughter. 'Goodnight, sweetheart. Sleep tight.'

And with a last wistful look at the blonde curls spread over the pink pillow she switched on the tiny lamp and left the room.

CHAPTER TEN

'MUMMY, Mummy, *he's been*.'

Bryony struggled upright in bed, watching as Lizzie dragged her stocking into the bedroom.

She looked for signs of disappointment but Lizzie's eyes were shining with excitement.

'This stocking is *so* lumpy. Can I eat chocolate for breakfast?' She giggled deliciously as she poked and prodded and Bryony smiled.

'I suppose so. Come into bed and we'll open it together.'

'In a minute.' Lizzie dropped the stocking and sprinted out of the room. 'I've got to find my daddy first.'

Bryony sank back against the pillows and gave a groan. 'Lizzie, I've already tried to tell you, there won't be a daddy.'

'Well, not in my stocking,' Lizzie called back, 'because no daddy would fit in there, silly. I'm going to look under the tree.'

Bryony closed her eyes, listening to the patter of feet as her child raced downstairs, and she braced herself for Lizzie's disappointment. It was perfectly obvious that all the dolls in the world weren't going to make up for not having a daddy on Christmas day.

She should have tried harder.

She should have used a dating agency or gone speed-dating.

She should have tried *anything*.

Deciding that she'd better go downstairs and comfort Lizzie, she swung her legs out of bed and then heard a delighted squeal from the sitting room.

Bryony froze. What could Lizzie have possibly found underneath the tree that excited her so much?

Maybe the doll was a hit after all.

And then she heard a laugh. A deep, male laugh that she would have recognised anywhere.

Jack?

Hardly able to breathe, she tiptoed to the top of the stairs and peeped down, a frown touching her brows as she saw Jack sprawled on the carpet under her Christmas tree, talking softly to Lizzie who was sitting on him, giggling with excitement.

'Jack?' Bryony walked down the stairs, holding the bannister tightly. 'What are you doing here? Why are you lying under my Christmas tree?'

He sat up, his blue gaze curiously intent as he looked at her.

'Because that's where Christmas presents are supposed to be.' His voice was husky and he gave her a lopsided smile. 'And I'm Lizzie's Christmas present.'

Bryony felt a thrill of hope deep inside her and then she buried it quickly. Lizzie's Christmas present. Of course. He was doing this because he couldn't bear to see Lizzie disappointed. But that wasn't going to work, was it? Sooner or later he'd have to confess to Lizzie that it wasn't real.

'Jack.' Her tone was urgent but he simply smiled at her and then sat up, still holding Lizzie on his lap. He reached under the tree and handed the little girl a beautifully wrapped box.

'And because I couldn't exactly wrap myself up, I wrapped this up instead.'

Lizzie fell on it with a squeal of delight. 'It's for me?'

'Certainly it's for you.' His gaze slid back to Bryony, who was standing on the bottom step, unable to move. She wanted to know what was going on.

Lizzie tore the paper off the present and then gave a gasp of delight, holding up a silk dress in a beautiful shade of pink. 'Oh, and matching shoes. And a new tiara.'

Jack's eyes were on Bryony. 'Someone once told me that a little girl could never have too many tiaras,' he said softly, a strange light in his eyes. 'And that's the sort of thing you need to know if you're going to be a decent daddy.'

Bryony gave a faltering smile and looked at the dress her daughter was holding.

It looked like…

'It's a lovely dress, Jack,' Lizzie said wistfully, stroking it with her hand. 'Can I wear it now?'

Jack shook his head. 'But you can wear it soon. Or at least I hope you can. Do you know what sort of dress this is, Lizzie?'

Lizzie shook her head but Bryony's heart was thumping like a drum and she sat down hard on the bottom stair as her knees gave way.

'It's a bridesmaid's dress,' Jack said quietly, his eyes still fixed on Bryony. 'And I want you to wear it when I marry your mummy.'

'You're going to marry Mummy?' Lizzie gave a gasp of delight. 'You're going to play Weddings?'

Jack gently tipped Lizzie onto the floor and rose to

his feet. 'I'm not playing Weddings,' he said quietly, walking across the room towards Bryony, his eyes locked on hers. 'I'm doing it for real.'

He reached into his pocket and pulled out a tiny box beautifully wrapped in silver paper. It caught the light and glittered like the decorations on the tree, and Lizzie gasped.

'It's so pretty.'

Bryony was looking at Jack and he smiled.

'Are you going to stand up?'

She took his hand and allowed him to pull her to her feet. 'Jack—'

'Bryony Hunter.' His voice was sexy and seductive and a tiny smile played around his firm mouth. 'Will you marry me?'

Her stomach turned over and she stared at him, not daring to believe that this was real. Then she looked at her daughter who was leaping up and down in undisguised delight.

Bryony took a deep breath and looked at the box. 'Jack—you don't want to get married. You were never going to get married,' she began, and he pressed the box into her hand.

'Sometimes I make mistakes, remember?' He winked at her and she rolled her eyes.

'I know, I know. Mistakes stop you from being perfect.'

'Precisely.' His voice was a velvet drawl. 'Open it, Blondie.'

'Yes, open it, Mummy!' Lizzie danced next to them and Bryony pulled the paper off with shaking fingers and stared down at the blue velvet box.

'It *can't* be a tiara,' Lizzie breathed and Bryony smiled.

'You think not?' Her eyes slid to Jack's and then back to the box again and she took a deep breath and flipped it open.

'Oh, Mummy!' Lizzie gasped in awe as the enormous diamond twinkled, reflecting the lights from the Christmas tree. 'That's *beautiful*.'

'It is beautiful.' She swallowed hard and looked at Jack. 'How—? Why—?'

Jack's gaze lingered on hers for her moment and then he turned to Lizzie. 'On second thought, why don't you go up to your bedroom and try the dress on?' he suggested. 'Then we can check if it fits.'

Without questioning him, Lizzie darted up the stairs and Bryony was left alone with Jack.

Her heart was racing and she felt strange inside but she still didn't dare believe that this was real.

'You've made her Christmas, Jack.' She looked after her daughter, her heart in her mouth, not knowing what to make of the situation. 'But you can't get married just for a child.'

'I didn't do it for Lizzie, Bryony,' he said softly, taking her face in his hands and forcing her to look at him. 'I did it for me. And for you.'

She tried not to look at his incredibly sexy mouth. 'You don't want commitment,' she croaked. 'You don't do for ever.'

'I didn't think I did, but I was wrong.'

She shook her head, forcing herself to say what needed to be said, despite the temptation just to take what she'd been given without question. 'There's only one reason to get married, Jack, and it isn't to please a child.'

'I know there's only one reason to get married,' he said hoarsely, stroking her blonde hair back from her face with a gentle hand. 'In fact, I know that better than anyone because I saw my parents together for all the wrong reasons.'

She looked at him, her mouth dry. 'So what's the reason, Jack?'

He bent his head and his mouth hovered close to hers. 'I'm marrying you because I love you,' he said softly. 'And why it's taken me so long to work that out I really don't know.'

She stood still, unable to believe that he'd actually said those words. And then a warm glow began inside her. 'You love me.'

He gave her that lopsided smile that always made her insides go funny. 'You know I love you. You were the one who told me that I love you.'

'And I seem to remember that you ran away from me so fast you left skid marks in the snow.'

He grinned. 'I know. And I'm sorry about that.'

'Where did you go?'

'I went back to my house.'

She looked at him in surprise. 'Your house? But you hardly ever go there.'

'I know that.' He pulled a face. 'Which is ridiculous really because it's a beautiful house with lots of land and a great view.'

'But it's never been a home for you, has it?' she said quietly, and he shook his head.

'No, it hasn't. And you're one of the few people that understand that.' He looked deep into her eyes. 'I went home and I sat in that house and I thought about all the years that I'd been miserable there. And

I suddenly realised that home for me is nothing to do with beautiful houses and land. It's to do with people. Home for me is where you are, Bryony, and it always has been.'

She swallowed hard. 'Jack—'

'I was scared of commitment, of having a marriage that was like my parents', but we are nothing like my parents.' He pulled her into his arms. 'The other night, when you said you'd loved me for ever, was it true?'

She nodded. 'Completely true.'

He let out a breath. 'And I've loved you for ever, too. But I associated marriage with disaster so I didn't want to take that risk with our relationship.'

'There's no risk, Jack.' She smiled up at him. 'Lizzie and I will always be here for you.'

'And I for you.' He released her and took the box out of her hand. 'This says that you're mine. For ever. No more dating. No more looking for a man to take your mind off me. From now on I want your mind well and truly *on* me. All the time.'

She gave a shaky smile, watching as he slid the beautiful ring onto her finger. 'It's huge. I've just put on half a stone and I haven't eaten any turkey yet.'

His eyes dropped to her mouth. 'I love you, sweetheart.'

There was a noise from the stairs. 'This time Jack is *really* going to kiss you, Mummy, I can tell by the way he's looking at you. Sort of funny.'

Bryony rolled her eyes and pulled a face. 'Nothing is ever private,' she muttered, and Jack grinned.

'Oh, believe me, later on we're going to be very private.' He pulled her against him and kissed her gently, but it was a fairly chaste kiss, given that Lizzie was watching avidly, and Bryony was touched by that. He always did the right thing around her daughter.

She reached out a hand to Lizzie.

'So, angel, did Santa do well?'

Lizzie smiled, her whole face alight with happiness. 'I knew he'd do it if I gave him enough time. And just to make sure that I get what I want next year, I've just written my letter for next Christmas.'

Bryony looked at her in disbelief. 'Sweetheart, you haven't even eaten your turkey yet! You can't already be thinking about next Christmas.'

'I can.' Lizzie looked at them stubbornly and waved the letter under their noses. 'I know exactly what I want. And I know that if I'm *really* good Santa will give it to me. But he's going to need a lot of time to get ready for this one because it's *very* special.'

Bryony exchanged looks with Jack who swept Lizzie into his arms and gave her a hug, laughter in his eyes.

'Go on, then. What is it that you want from Santa next year?'

Lizzie smiled. 'Well…' she said, smiling into Jack's face and wrapping her little arms round his neck. 'For Christmas next year, I really *really* want a baby sister. And I *know* that Santa is going to bring me one.'

WE VALUE YOUR OPINION!

YOUR CHANCE TO WIN A ONE YEAR SUPPLY OF YOUR FAVOURITE BOOKS.

If you are a regular UK reader of Mills & Boon® Medical Romance™ and have always wanted to share your thoughts on the books you read—here's your chance:

Join the Reader Panel today!

This is your opportunity to let us know exactly what you think of the books you love.

And there's another great reason to join:

Each month, all members of the Reader Panel have a chance of winning four of their favourite Mills & Boon romance books EVERY month for a whole year!

If you would like to be considered for the Reader Panel, please complete and return the following application. Unfortunately, as we have limited spaces, we cannot guarantee that everyone will be selected.

Name: _____

Address: _____

_____ Post Code: _____

Home Telephone: _____ Email Address: _____

Where do you normally get your Mills & Boon Medical Romance books (please tick one of the following)?

Shops ❑ Library/Borrowed ❑

Reader Service™ ❑ If so, please give us your subscription no. _____

Please indicate which age group you are in:

16 – 24 ❑ 25 – 34 ❑

35 – 49 ❑ 50 – 64 ❑ 65 + ❑

If you would like to apply by telephone, please call our friendly Customer Relations line on **020 8288 2886**, or get in touch by email to readerpanel@hmb.co.uk

Don't delay, apply to join the Reader Panel today and help ensure the range and quality of the books you enjoy.

Send your application to:

The Reader Service, Reader Panel Questionnaire, FREEPOST NAT1098, Richmond, TW9 1BR

If you do not wish to receive any additional marketing material from us, please contact the Data Manager at the address above.

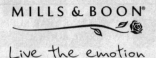

FREE

4 BOOKS AND A SURPRISE GIFT!

We would like to take this opportunity to thank you for reading this Mills & Boon® book by offering you the chance to take FOUR more specially selected titles from the Medical Romance™ series absolutely FREE! We're also making this offer to introduce you to the benefits of the Reader Service™—

> ★ **FREE home delivery**
> ★ **FREE gifts and competitions**
> ★ **FREE monthly Newsletter**
> ★ **Books available before they're in the shops**
> ★ **Exclusive Reader Service offers**

Accepting these FREE books and gift places you under no obligation to buy; you may cancel at any time, even after receiving your free shipment. Simply complete your details below and return the entire page to the address below. You don't even need a stamp!

YES! Please send me 4 free Medical Romance books and a surprise gift. I understand that unless you hear from me, I will receive 6 superb new titles every month for just £2.69 each, postage and packing free. I am under no obligation to purchase any books and may cancel my subscription at any time. The free books and gift will be mine to keep in any case.

M4ZEE

Ms/Mrs/Miss/Mr......................................Initials ....
                                                                    BLOCK CAPITALS PLEASE

Surname ....

Address ....

....

....Postcode ....

Send this whole page to:
The Reader Service, FREEPOST CN81, Croydon, CR9 3WZ